TWENTY-EIGHT places on his body leaking blood, yet he continued to fight and load his wounded comrades on the extraction slick. He was blinded by blood from shrapnel embedded so deep in his head, neck and face that he cut his hands while trying to wipe the blood away. A round from an AK-47 had entered his lower back on the right, missed his heart by a few millimeters, and exited under his left armpit. It had opened a hole so wide his intestines were trying to squeeze out from the tear that jutted almost to his stomach. He couldn't speak intelligibly either; an enemy rifle butt broke teeth and snapped his jaw shut. The bayonet slashes in his right arm were to the bone, but his left arm took the most damage. It looked as if it had been ripped by a chainsaw. And another round, the first hit he took, went through his right calf. A second - or was it the third - lodged in his left leg just below his scrotum. The other two slaps he felt were bullets in the back of his upper right leg, just below the buttocks. These would have been enough to stop anyone - well almost anyone - but not this Green Beret Sergeant with a will of steel and a lean, muscled body carved out of granite.

Roy Benavidez was a combat veteran. He forced himself onward - never to quit. He explains that it was his duty. I say it was a combination of adrenalin, courage, the driving force that compels him to win - to excel - his strong belief in the Lord, and a realization that others needed him. Plus the code he lived by then and lives by now, the one he "borrowed" from West Point:

DUTY - HONOR - COUNTRY.

959.7   3899
Billac

The last medal of honor.

DATE DUE

959.7		3899
CLASS		ACC
Billac.		
(LAST NAME OF AUTHOR)		
The last medal of honor.		
(BOOK TITLE)		
DATE DUE	ISSUED TO	
AP 09 '95	DyKE RASCO	

First Baptist Church Library
Tomball, Texas

THE
LAST MEDAL OF HONOR

By

Pete Billac

Peace Always—
Roy P. Benavidez (MoH)
Duty Honor Country

Swan Publishers
New York * Texas * California

FIRST BAPTIST CHURCH LIBRARY
TOMBALL, TEXAS

OTHER WORKS BY THE AUTHOR

Beneath the Gulf
The Acquiescent Wanderer
Alfredo
The Annihilator
How Not to be Lonely
A Woman's Life After Divorce
Hot to Handle a Macho Man
Living and Loving Past the Big 5-0
How Not to be Lonely...TONIGHT

Copyright @ 1990 by Pete Billac
Library of Congress Catalog Number 90-70069
ISBN 0-943629-07-7

All rights reserved. No part of this book may be reproduced or transmitted in any form or by any means, electronic or mechanical, including photocopying, recording, or by any information storage or receival system without permission in writing from the author.

THE LAST MEDAL OF HONOR is available in quantity discounts. Please address inquiries to SWAN PUBLISHING CO. P.O. Box 580242, Houston, TX 77258

Printed in the United States of America

DEDICATION

This book is dedicated to the memory of the American war veterans. And to the homeless veterans and those in hospitals, clinics, and aid stations all over the world. Also to those who are at home but have a hard time sleeping or being able to cope with life because of the battles they fought. I understand you most of all.

And to the nurses, who seem to have been forgotten. You ladies were special, and I thank God you were there for me and the tens of thousands of others who needed you so desperately.

Finally, to the veterans who gave up their tomorrow so each of us could live our todays.

ROY P. BENAVIDEZ

ACKNOWLEDGEMENTS

Many people contributed to the information in this book. I will try to thank them all.

First, to ROY BENAVIDEZ for his countless hours of being interviewed; his tapes, letters, telephone calls, photographs, and his 160-mile roundtrip drives to visit with me, his many books and newspaper articles and his patience. Without his input - and certainly his will to survive the Vietnam war - this book could never have become a reality.

Thanks also to John and Michael Pepe. John is the president of Polaris Entertainment Company, and Michael, an engineer. Their many hours of editing, suggestions and help in typesetting need to be recognized. And to my editor and publicist, Sharon Davis, and certainly to Dr. Frank Reuter for his final editing and correcting.

To Andy Alder for his graphic work, to Al and Norma Davis, Gene Buckle and Ab Webber for their financial aid and to those who were in some way responsible for getting us all to this point in life.

Space limits what I can say about the following individuals and they will not be listed in alphabetical order:
Mrs. Eve Bartlett; Charles E. Brown; Dr. Ronald Goelzer; Cy Stapleton; Bo Griffin; Hector Garcia; Emmett Shelton, Jr.; Emmett Shelton, Sr.; I.J. Irvin, Jr.; Sergeant Major Robert (Moe) Canales; John P. Charlton, Inspector General with DAV; Mr. and Mrs. A.E. Craig; Dean Allen; Bill Hydman; Stan Smith; Cris Gomez (SF); Jose Garcia; Raf Habeeb, NCOA (SF); MSg. Oved Guajardo (SF); Maj. Fred Jones (SF); SSM Joe Lopez (SF); Brigadier General Herbert Lloyd (SF); CSM Larry Martin (SF); Wade McMackins (SF); Jose Moreno; Bernie Newson; Jim Mason,

(Vietnam pilot); Dr. Bill Moser (SF); Ron Siegman, (SF); Texas Senator Frank Tejada; Steve Sucher; David Vela; Jake and Mildred Woodruff; Dale Roberson; Raymond Vela; CSM Harry Ward (SF); CWO Ruben Salazar (SF); David Erbstoesser; Major Bob Garcia; Alfredo Garza; SFC Martin G. Gloria; Lieutenant Colonel Charles Kettles (chopper pilot); Jorge Lomelia (SF); Frank W. Stransky (SF); Herb Norch (CPO); Lieutenant Colonel Bob Chisolm (Airborne); Allen Schoppe (Airborne); Cruz S. Chavira; Bob Gibson; Joe Galindo; SGM Louis Pineda (82nd); Jo and Effort Hart; SGM Benito Guerrero; CSM Ed Miller (SF); and Dr. Hector Garcia.

Murry Fathergill, Jack Goldman, Congressman Greg Laughlin; "Chargin' Charlie" Beckwith; Dr. Hugh Ratliff; Jack Ingram; CMS A.J Walker; Jim Springer; Pete Sutton; Tom Gloria; Norma Linda Martinez; Eduardo Villejo and Allen Clark.

And a special thanks to the chopper pilots, the TAC officer and pilots and the men who risked (and gave) their lives so that Roy Benavidez could help after his war. Yeah, guys like Jesse Naul, Jerry Ewing, Larry McKibben, Hoffman, Fussell, Smith, Fernan, Darling, "Frenchy" Mousseau, Leroy Wright, Brian O'Connor and Waggie; to Colonel Ralph Drake, Armstrong, General Tornow and "Ski", and to the nurses and doctors who gave so much and saved so many. And thanks to the Lord for making it possible for Roy to be here and for me to be able to write this wonderful story on the recipient of **THE LAST MEDAL OF HONOR**.

CONTENTS

PART I

THE BATTLE

First Meeting	17
Loc Ninh, Vietnam May 2nd, 1968	23
Going In	27
The McGuire Rig	31
O'Connor's Story	33
The Forward Air Controller	47
Six Hours in Hell	53
Roger Waggie	61
Mano a Mano	69

PART II

NOT SUPPOSED TO DIE

Buried Alive 77

Another Close Call 81

The Distinguished Service Cross 87

The Hospital 89

Receiving The Medal of Honor 91

Always a Soldier 97

Hello, Remember Me? 101

PART III

HEROES

Roger Donlon 105

History of The Medal of Honor 111

A Woman Receives The Medal 115

Sergeant York 119

MacArthur Gets The Medal 125

Audie Murphy 127

Captain Samuel Fuqua 131

Custer 133

Clarence Sasser 135

David Cantu Barkley 137

Sergeant John Pittman 139

PART IV

AFTER THE WAR

Roy's War Ends 141

Why I Fought in Vietnam 143

Another War 149

Hero Street 153

Martha Raye 155

A Letter to President Bush 159

Captain Daniel Castillo 163

Jerry Cottingham 167

Isaac George Rodriguez 169

Barry Sadler 171

"Mad Dog" Shriver 173

PART V

WRAPPING IT UP

Young Americans 175

Letters to Roy 181

Roy's Awards and Decorations 189

Honors 191

Epilog 193

Bibliography 201

Glossary 209

PREFACE

How do I begin telling you about a man who has become a living legend? How can I possibly tell you more than what you read on the that first page as you opened this book? I know, I'll tell you of the actual battle, in detail.

I forewarn you, this combat story is not for the faint-at-heart. It is frighteningly candid, bloody - gory even - almost unbelievable. It is a small part of a real war, and I tell it to the best of my ability.

This battle sequence is from a compilation of facts and events taken from personal interviews, telephone conversations, and numerous letters and stories written about this particular event. It is from information written for and signed by Ronald Reagan, then-President of the United States. And, it is this authors' interpretation of what actually happened, taken from these facts.

This particular story is based on one event that took place on May 2nd, 1968, in a section of Cambodia just 15 klicks (kilometers) west of the South Vietnamese village of Loc Ninh.

Allied troops were not supposed to be in that area but we *were* there. Everyone connected with the war knew we were there, but we didn't want to admit it at the time. Now, we can tell it the way it was.

Personally, I never did understand these rules. The North Vietnamese Army (the NVA) and the Viet Cong (Vietnamese Communist or VC) were "allowed" to come on "our" side from Cambodia and Laos, but we were not allowed to go on *their* side. Doesn't that sound a bit unfair? It was unfair and it was stupid and after many of our troops were killed by these VC or NVA who could run to their side to safety, that "rule" was changed. Some of what Roy and the other Special Forces team accomplished that day was responsible for that change in rules.

The CIA got involved and formed SOG teams - Special Operations Groups - and we went over that safe line. Seems right, doesn't it? But for some strange reason we never wanted to admit we went over on their side; that we weren't stupid. I'll leave you with that thought. Perhaps the politicians can explain it.

Pete Billac

FIRST MEETING

From the first day I met Roy Benavidez, I liked him. He walked up to me, shook my hand and, introduced himself. His handshake was firm but friendly. He smiled and seemed cheerful, almost childlike. He walked with a limp, head bent slightly right and he was overweight.

Other men at an 82nd Airborne party where we met knew him, they shook his hand, and the men slapped backs and embraced each other. But he seemed to be the one they were waiting for. He didn't look like a hero to me; he looked like a fat, cheerful Mexican. But what does a hero look like? I can tell you here and now that they look like everybody. In appearance, they are no different than your grocer, mailman, or bank executive. They look like a college student, college professor, or a high school dropout. They are, however, special "inside."

Roy and I went to the lobby and talked. I told him he was the first Medal of Honor winner I had met. He looked me in the eye, a serious gaze. "I'm a *recipient* of the medal," he said. "I wasn't in a contest and I didn't 'win' the medal. It was awarded to me." He smiled. I smiled back. "You can win a Medal of Honor in a poker game. Those of us who have this medal like to be referred to as recipients." I've never forgotten that terminology.

As I talked to Roy, I discovered he was a regular person, someone like you and me, well, almost. He is Hispanic, an Hispanic/American he calls himself, of Yaqui Indian decent. And he is still a member of the military although retired since 1976. A prime example is, he shaves every day yet he has little facial hair. I asked him about this. "A good soldier, it states in the manual, should shave every day," he replied. He also gets one of those GI haircuts every Friday morning.

Roy makes speeches all over the world. He speaks to schools, civic organizations, veterans celebrations, and almost any group who asks when the group is close to where he lives. He drives a 1981 Chevy El Camino, with over 200,000 miles on the odometer. When he flies, he still has about a 180-mile roundtrip drive from his home in El Campo, Texas, to get to the closest airport.

Roy has a wife, Lala, and three children, Denise, 23, Yvette, 20, and a son, Noel, age 17. He lives in a modest house; he has a few changes of clothes and doesn't seem to be short on groceries. His medical bills are paid by the Veterans Administration; he receives full disability from the government - less than *half* the salary of a Los Angeles garbage man.

He stays on medication but he hurts - he hurts most of the hours in each day. When the weather changes and gets cold, he hurts more. He has a quarter-pound or so of metal still in his body. One neighbor complained that she sees him walking a few times each day. "Why shouldn't he work like the rest of us?"

I'd like her to know that he walks so he won't freeze up. As time passes, these torn muscles and ligaments and mounds of scar tissue become more of a problem and he must walk constantly to keep them loose.

Yet another complaint she voiced was, "she sees him on television and in the newspapers and hears him over the radio." This is part of what he is doing to help youngsters in grade school, high school and even college ROTC units understand that they can make a success in life without the use of drugs, alcohol or a family with means. He tells them, regardless of their situation, that they can become somebody if they try, if they learn, and if they use this knowledge. And he tells them about the horrors of war but also of the necessity of serving your country and making sacrifices.

Yes ma'am, he walks and he appears in the news. Why not be proud of him and of what he's doing - of what he has done? I guess I could never explain it to those who have not been there to understand the sacrifice Roy Benavidez made so we could all enjoy freedom. To those who feel he is getting a "free ride on your tax money," I'd like you to live inside his body for a day or two. When he travels, oftentimes it is at his own expense and much of the time he's hurting, but he won't fail to make an appearance regardless of how much he hurts.

Lady, I want you to know that because of him and others like him, you are able to live and enjoy this country. Because of him you are "allowed" to work. Because of the blood he and his comrades shed for this country, you are able to complain. Because these special people gave their tomorrow, you are able to enjoy your todays.

He has so much metal in his body that the alarm rings at the airport. I spent a few nights in the same hotel room with him, and he gets up at least four or five times a night because he gets stiff and he hurts - he hurts bad.

We were having dinner one evening and I noticed him picking at his nose. "Don't do that you illbred wetback," I joked in a whisper. (I'm allowed to kid him this way because my mother's maiden name is *Hernandez*.) "Go to the bathroom to do that, or stick you head under the table. What kind of role-model are you for kids, sitting in a public restaurant and picking boogers from your nose?"

He smiled and put a napkin to his nose to blot the blood. "*Look at this,*" he said. "*This darn piece of metal has been working its way down and just came out.*" He showed me a small *sliver* of metal, one of the many lodged in his body from that fateful date in 1968 when he was sprayed by mortar fire. In fact, two more of these "slivers" of metal are trying to work their way from his body, one in his forehead right at the hairline and another just above his right wrist.

All I could do was smile, sigh deeply, and feel quietly embarrassed. This incident motivated me to write his story. It should be told. It needs to be read by adults and children, veterans who tasted battle and witnessed death and those who served but never saw action.

I'm writing this story because people need to know about this courageous person. I'm writing it because there is a story to be told *after* the Medal of Honor. And I'm writing it because Roy wants kids all over the world to know that regardless of their circumstances, their color, religion, background, financial status, education or bad breaks, they too can excel.

Roy Perez Benavidez wants to show others that a Mexican kid born in Cuero, Texas, the son of a sharecropper who died when Roy was two year old, a kid who lived with his uncle and 8 other kids, a kid who picked cotton and was discriminated against in school and who dropped out of school in 7th grade, can make it if he tries. Roy wants all such kids to believe in themselves, in the good Lord, and to get an education and TRY!

A percentage of the proceeds from this book will go directly to the Homeless Vietnam Veterans and the Nurses Memorial. Roy demands it!

Now, let's get on with the action. Let's tell the entire story of that day, those six-hours in hell, the day that has changed Roy's entire life.

Roy in jump school with 82nd Airborne at Fort Bragg, N.C. in 1959, his first step to become a Green Beret.

Special Forces camp in Vietnam, heavily fortified with punji stakes, concertina wire and mines.

LOC NINH, VIETNAM MAY 2nd, 1968

   Roy Benavidez was where he wanted to be. Was he insane? Vietnam was no beach resort, quite the contrary. It was a hellhole. It was hot and steamy during the day and cold at night. There were bugs and insects of all types that stung without warning. And it was blood and death!
   But Roy - Staff Sergeant Benavidez - knew all of that. He was there because he believed his country needed him to combat the advance of communism. He had been a member of the 82nd Airborne Division; he was now a Green Beret, in Special Forces, a member of America's most elite fighting group.
   The morning was already pouring sweltering heat throughout the jungle but Sergeant Benavidez was tucked away in the moderate safety of his tent at Loch Ninh, a small speck on the map of South Vietnam, just a hairsbreadth from the Cambodian border.
   Droplets of water from the overnight rain made a disturbing patter on the wooden floor of his tent and he stretched, laced his boots and, already dressed in Tiger Stripe fatigues, walked toward the mess hall.
   He stopped at the communications tent to see if anything was going on that he should know about. He knew a secret mission three of his Special Forces comrades were going on was scheduled that very morning.
   The radio was making funny noises, static maybe, no... automatic weapon fire and the sound of mortars! Voices too, voices that were screaming in frustration and cursing the situation.
   Roy ran from the tent toward the airstrip. He knew if anything was happening, the airstrip was the place to find out about it. A helicopter gunship had gone down in the jungle and the crew was being picked up by Warrant Office

Larry McKibben's extraction slick. Roy stood and watched the helicopter come in - quickly and hard.

As McKibben's chopper landed, the rescued crew began to pour out. A second chopper was coming in, piloted by Warrant Officers Hoffman and Waggie. Each chopper was shot up, but that second slick had holes in almost every inch of the craft. "How in the world could anyone survive *that*?" Roy thought.

Roy went to the second chopper and saw Craig, the 19-year old doorgunner from Rosemeade, California. He was hit bad. In desperation and hope, Roy helped lower the wounded airman to the ground and cradled him in his arms.

Craig died. His last words were "*Oh my God, my mother and father...*" and he was gone. Roy's eyes closed, tears squeezing from them. He got to his feet and tried not to think of anything. He had seen men die before. He had seen boys die before. But Craig was so young, a special kid. Roy liked him.

McKibben's chopper was going back in to get the team he had dropped off earlier. They were in trouble. Roy learned that it was three of his comrades, the three who were on a secret mission: Wright, Mousseau and O'Connor, along with 9 CIDG's, (Civilian Irregular Defense Group) Vietnamese civilians who fought with the US against the NVA and VC.

With a jump-start from the battery of Waggie's chopper, the turbines on McKibben's slick began to whine and the huge blades made their familiar *whup-whup* sounds, slicing echoes through the thick jungle air. Roy, knowing the importance of the mission, jumped aboard.

In talking to Roy, I asked him why he had done such a foolhardy thing? What could he do? How did he plan to help? Radio reports had an entire *battalion* of NVA down there, at least 200 men, maybe more. The area was hot. Roy had no weapon other than his Special Forces knife and a bag of medical supplies.

"I did it from instinct, I guess," Roy told me. "I knew the mission was important. Vehicles, arms, and troops were making their way through Cambodia and we needed information to prove it so we could cross the boundary *into* Cambodia. Our guys had papers, maps, maybe photos in their possession. If they had taken these photos, we needed them as proof that the VC and NVA were, in fact, using this safe zone to transport their war supplies. Each team leader also carried a chart of the radio frequencies for the day. If the enemy got those, they could use our frequencies to call incorrect information like TAC or gunships, maybe extraction choppers where they weren't needed and annihilate our guys. Someone had to make certain these documents were secure and, from the sound of the cries over the radio, our team was desperate. I felt I could make certain the papers were safe and help rescue my comrades too, my three SF buddies and the 9 CIDG's. I think I acted first from instinct then thought about it later," he said. "Matter of fact, it had to be instinct," he smiled. "*Involuntary Reflex Action*, psychologists call it."

"Yeah, that was it. Involuntary reflex action." His smile broadened. "I wasn't nuts either," he said as he looked at me. "I was Special Forces. We were trained to aid our comrades at all costs. You know," he sighed, "I guess I didn't think. I just did what I was trained to do. The mission was secret so it had to be important, and I knew that those SOI papers could not fall into the wrong hands. At the time," Roy sighed, "I reacted. I had to get the papers first, my comrades next," he signed deeply again, "and I guess, get out alive. But, I don't think I ever thought about dying, just doing my duty."

And knowing him, I believe him. He thought that way then and he thinks that way now. His "borrowed" code from West Point, DUTY - HONOR - COUNTRY, took priority over all else. He believes in it, he follows it, and he acted that day in Loc Ninh *because* of it.

Mike Craig, 19-year old helicopter doorgunner who died in Roy's arms, May 2nd, 1968.

GOING IN

It surely was a "hot" zone down there. Reports indicated 300 or more - maybe 350 NVA, the North Vietnam Army, no rag-tag outfit but trained army combat soldiers.

As McKibben's slick descended toward an opening, his doorgunners were cutting lose with their M-60 machine guns, raking the jungle from one side to another with 7.62 mm tumblers at 500 rounds per minute, covering all four points. The chopper hovered for a split second about 10 feet off the ground. Roy grabbed the bag of medical supplies, threw it out, then jumped, doing a paratrooper landing fall as his body touched ground.

"I was standing in tall grass. McKibben flew out over the team's position and I ran along behind him. I had run maybe twenty - five or so yards when I felt a thorn tear at my pant leg at my calf. A flash of pain ran up my leg. I ran a few more feet then dropped to the ground. I called out to Leroy, the team leader. There wasn't a reply. I reached down to where I thought the thorn had nicked me and put my finger in a deep hole in my right calf. I looked at it, saw the blood and looked at the other side. There was a hole there too! I had been shot!"

"Ben...is that you?" It was Mousseau calling to me. He wasn't that far away, maybe ten or so yards. I got up to run and fell, rolled a few times, tried to run, fell again, and crawled to Mousseau's side."

The NVA apparently hadn't seen Roy - they were shooting wildly in the grass - and didn't know the *exact* position of the team members. The bullets were nipping all around him like angry hornets. Roy was lying on the ground, face in the dirt. When he looked up at Mousseau, he winced at what he saw.

"There was blood everywhere," Roy told me. "Here were six men in a huddle, Mousseau propped against a tree. He had taken a round in the shoulder, one in the stomach, and his left eye was dangling from a head wound. His eyeball was sticking out, hanging from a thread of meat. I could see the empty socket. But he was still fighting, still firing, still acutely aware of what was going on. I patched him up the best I could, and went to look at the others.

"The five CIDG's with him were also battered. I tended to their wounds then positioned them facing the area of the PZ, the pickup zone, where Mousseau said the rest of the team were hidden."

Roy took Mousseau's emergency radio and called to McKibben, who acknowledged the call and was coming in for extraction. Roy told the men to get ready to get out of there. Then, lifting his head above the grass, he spotted O'Connor maybe 20 feet away. He forgot about the bullet hole through his calf.

Bullets were zinging all over the place. The smoke was so thick you could hardly see and the constant chattering of automatic weapons played a monotonous tune as bullets sliced through the grass and ricocheted off trees. Since the NVA didn't know exactly where they were, they just saturated the area with small arms fire, mortars and automatic weapon fire.

As Roy called out to O'Connor asking how he was, O'Connor gave him a thumbs up, meaning he was alive. But barely. O'Connor raised two fingers when Roy asked how many others were alive. That meant four were missing. And that was when Roy recalled his thoughts went to the SOI papers Leroy Wright had, the Special Operating Instructions, maps, and other secret material that had to be brought back.

That was the reason for the entire mission. Yeah, the mission was of greater importance than the men *on* the mission. The right information meant thousands of lives could be saved. If there were photos to retrieve, it meant we could then go into Cambodia. No more shooting our guys in ambush then getting away clean to escape to some Cambodian refuge. And the last thing the team leader would dispose of would be those photos as well as the radio frequencies. He needed the call letters to call for extraction. We couldn't let those get in enemy hands. Special Forces training was ruling. Roy had to get to Leroy Wright to get those papers.

Yeah, Roy wanted to get the Special Operating Instructions from Leroy's pocket, but he also wanted to get Leroy Wright. He *owed* Leroy.

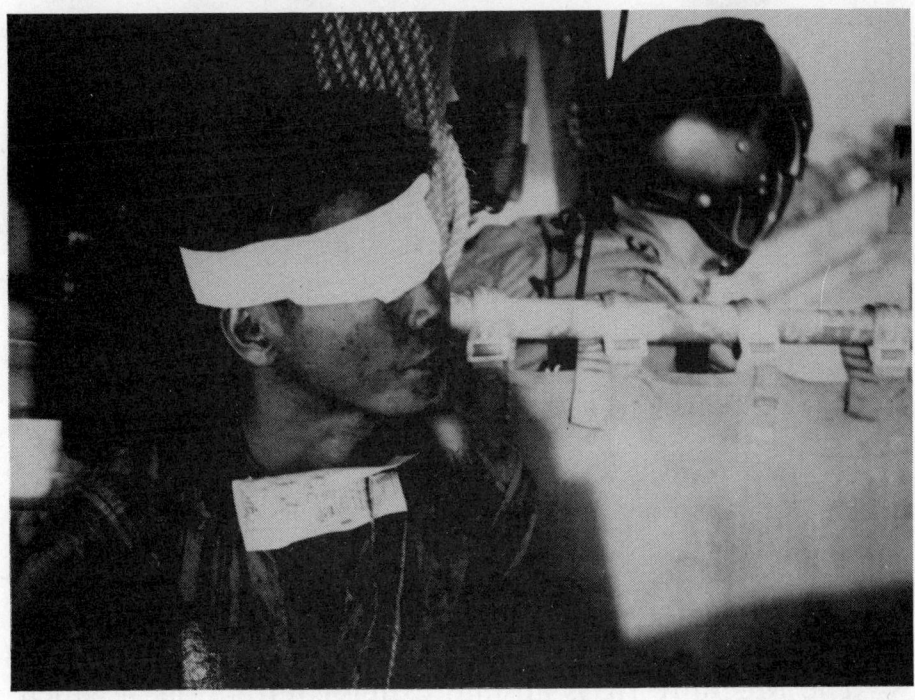

Viet Cong prisoner Roy captured and frightened into giving information by having him taste Tabasco sauce. He thought it was poison. It is!

The McGuire rig is an interesting contraption; a winch in the doorway of an extraction chopper, it suspends two nylon ropes and horseshoe webbing for a man to slip his head and shoulders through and straps to fit snugly under the armpits.

THE McGUIRE RIG

Leroy was special. Roy and Leroy had several things in common because of their backgrounds. Leroy was *African - American*; Roy was *Hispanic-American*. Both had suffered discrimination and racism in their youth. Each knew how the other felt, they talked about it at Bragg. And because of being Green Berets, they were brothers. *All* SF guys feel that way. Roy had two reasons to get to Leroy...no, three. He also owed his life to Leroy. He'd get Leroy *and* the papers.

A few weeks earlier Roy was part of a two-man *Special Forces* team was inserted into the jungle on a routine reconnaissance mission. They were detected, fighting began, and the battle heated. They called for extraction and the slick came but, the jungle was too thick to land a chopper so the two Green Berets, Benavidez and Fields, were to be lifted by a McGuire rig.

Each extraction slick has a bellyman - a guy who operates the McGuire. He lays on his belly on the floor of the chopper and works the winch lifting people into the chopper. He sticks his head out from the open door to see what he's doing, and he must keep those nylon ropes from tangling or rubbing together. With the weight of two troopers if the lines rubbed, they would probably catch fire, and the two guys would plunge back into the jungle - without benefit of a parachute.

"This particular day when Leroy and I got closer in our relationship was when I was being lifted on one of the ropes on the McGuire and Jerry Fields on the other. Small arms fire was zinging around us and pelting the sides and underbelly of the chopper.

"I began to twist in my rig, looking down and to all sides to see where the firing was coming from. Our ropes tangled. The helicopter had us up about 500 feet when the ropes began to smoke. We were about 20 feet from the open door and the rig chugged to a halt, lines heating as we hung, rubbing and grinding, as the bellyman strained to pull us up to safety. A completely helpless feeling to say the least.

"As I looked up, I saw Leroy stick his head out. He had half of his body out of the chopper now, leaning over, trying to reach the lines and separate them, while bullets were being fired up at him from the jungle below. Leroy Wright, that fine, black, Special Forces friend of mine from Fort Bragg, had his *feet* tied with ropes and his entire body was exposed to the firing below. He was risking his life to save mine.

"Leroy separated the lines, and I felt his strong arms pull me into the chopper. Yeah, Leroy had saved my life and now was my time to repay the debt."

Combat hardened - Battle ready

O'CONNOR'S STORY

O'Connor had been on the ground over an hour fighting, getting hit, and seeing his comrades being wounded and dying at the hands of the NVA before Roy arrived. He was calling out to his CIDG interpreter for more ammo and grenades. Roy yelled for O'Connor to come over to his position, that the slick with McKibben at the controls was coming in to get them. O'Connor had taken a burst of an automatic weapon in his stomach, another hit in his right thigh and a third wound in his left ankle. A fourth bullet pierced his left arm.

O'Connor tried to crawl toward Roy with the lone CIDG in tow. The other two CIDG's were finished. As O'Connor, nicknamed *Big Team*, made his move the NVA opened fire, bullets raining in the trees surrounding them and cutting through the heavy grass. Roy was standing, reaching out to help O'Connor when he felt a jolt in his right thigh that felt like a bowling ball had been dropped from the sky and landed on his leg. He fell back as second round slapped into him, on his right buttocks, he believed. He felt yet another one or two hits thud into an already-numb right leg; he lay on his back trying to decide what to do.

"All I remember was getting hit and feeling numb," Roy said. "The pain began to spread. It felt like a hot fire was burning on top of me. I thought of the slick and McKibben and hoped I'd be able to walk. But then I thought about Leroy. Where was he? He had the SOI papers. Gotta get to Leroy."

But Leroy was not able to answer or to see that a chopper was coming in to rescue them. He fought heroically but he had taken too many hits. No, Leroy couldn't answer. Leroy was dead.

O'Connor wrote an 8-page letter to then-President of the United States, Ronald Reagan. He described his mission to the best of his recollection, including Roy's contribution to the extraction.

"Early on the morning of May 2nd, 1968, I was part of a Special Forces team set to leave from Quon Loi, South Vietnam, headquarters for the First Brigade of the First Infantry Division. Quon Loi is approximately five miles southeast from Loc Ninh, where the Special Forces base was tucked neatly in the jungle, on the south side of the Cambodian border.

"The mission was to gather information and get it back to headquarters. We were to avoid contact with the enemy, just get information. But it didn't work that way.

"Special Forces operated in teams, usually 5 to 10 men depending on the call. On this mission, Sergeant First Class Leroy Wright was the TL, our team leader, Sergeant Senior Grade Floyd "*Frenchy*" Mousseau was the ATL, our assistant team leader, and SP-4 Brian O'Connor, the radioman. Along with the team of the three Special Forces soldiers there were nine CIDG's that included two interpreters.

"We made a silent insertion by two slicks with gunship backup west of Loc Ninh into a small LZ (landing zone) in Cambodia. I always get a rise when they use the word 'silent.' What in the world is ever silent about a helicopter? But the chopper pilots did the best they could. They would fly zig-zag routes, rising and lowering in the trees, darting in and out of clouds, shadows - anything to throw whoever might be monitoring from being able to pinpoint an insertion.

"This morning was no different than the rest. We usually took off at early light and watched the sun rise, lighting up the darkness below. And one spot looked like the other - trees, tall grass, an opening. We could rarely spot movement below, until of course, as had happened many times before, we cruised in at the wrong spot and the jungles would come alive with hostile weapon fire.

"Although today was a secret mission, we were flying into Cambodia and a gunship accompanied us in case we ran into trouble before our *silent* insertion was made.

"As the chopper touched down, we ran toward the safety of the nearby woodbine where we took head count and equipment check. Leroy made radio contact signaling 'insertion completed.'

"The team leader decided we'd just lie still for a half hour or so to see if the insertion had, in fact, been without warning to the NVA. We took this time to plan the next leg of our mission. We knew it well but there were always *things* that would happen to alter the original plan.

"After about thirty minutes of observation and lying on the wet ground, listening for noises other than the chatter of monkeys and birds, we agreed to begin to move slowly toward the objective.

"The ATL, Mousseau, was walking point, Wright was centered, and I was tailgunner. We headed through the thicker woods slowly, circumventing the LZ until we came across the designated trail. Reaching it, Mousseau stopped to monitor it for traffic, then signaled me forward and whispered that three or more, maybe as many a five, of the enemy were coming down the trail. I signaled to the CIDG's to be quiet and let them pass. We were concerned with gathering information and wouldn't get into a firefight if we could avoid it.

"The quiet was interrupted by branches cracking, the sound of a brief scuffle, muffled screams and a short burst of small arms fire. Wright, our team leader, signaled us to reverse about thirty meters through thick brush into a gully where we waited for the others to join us and regroup.

"Three Vietnamese woodcutters had been chopping out a path in the narrow spot of the trail when they stumbled into Mousseau and the CIDG point man. Our guys took them out with knives but not before one of the woodcutters squeezed off a few rounds. *Our position had been compromised.*

"We waited in the thick growth and heard talking and yelling but couldn't determine what was being said. Wright tried to make contact with the FAC or the C & C (Forward Air Controller, or Command and Control helicopter that circled overhead to direct and coordinate air and ground operations) to call for possible extraction.

"We couldn't make contact so we proceeded to the first rally point to change antennas and try again. As we approached the rally point, we got a clear look at the LZ and could hear faint fading voices and the sound of brush being chopped at the far end of the LZ near the trail. Since we had not been detected, the team leader advised - and we agreed - to stay a while longer and try to accomplish our mission. The bodies had been dragged and hidden and who would miss three cutters, especially if there were dozens, we reasoned?

"Our CIDG interpreters were giving conflicting reports on what the enemy was saying. The CIDG who had been with me on other missions could not determine the size of troop concentration or whether they were VC or NVA or just an advance team of woodcutters.

"One interpreter said he thought they were NVA, maybe 10 or 12 strong, looking for either us or the downed helicopter, the chopper that was shot down less than a minute after it was airborne on the return to Loc Ninh, the crew

McKibben picked up earlier. The NVA had no idea what the chopper was doing or where it was coming from. We all agreed that the secrecy of our mission was still intact.

"Mousseau and I opened maps to determine if we would continue toward our objective or call for extraction. Wright made the decision. The objective was close and we had a one-time try. If we continued, chances are we could make a full report. If we had been discovered - compromised - or if we got into hot contact, we wouldn't be able to try again for days, weeks maybe. We knew the importance of our report. One day without this report could mean tons of weapons coming in that we could not - legally - stop.

"The returning noise from the far end of the LZ and increased activity on our side of the LZ quickly made us feel we *had* been compromised. Thoughts were leaping in and out of our minds in fractions of a second. We could read it in each others eyes. Leroy Wright nodded and we knew the decision was made. Wright called for immediate extraction. We'd have to abort the mission.

"The message was relayed and the reply came back that command wanted us to *continue* the mission. The TL said *'let's go'* and we took the short cut, me and a CIDG on point, Mousseau middle, and Wright as tail.

"We crossed a small open field and narrow roadway to get to the shortcut, and ran head-on into a dozen NVA regulars. Both units stopped in their tracks. We were all wearing tiger-striped fatigues and bush hats.

"Chin, our quick-thinking point man, began talking to their officer as I pulled a paper from my pocket and began to move toward Mousseau. We lowered our heads as if looking at a map to cover our round eyes. Our camouflage face paint helped with the color of our skin, but round eyes were a dead giveaway. We had to look down and do our best to avoid eye contact no matter how much we wanted to look to see what was going on. The interpreter moved past us and towards the point and told us they thought we might be another unit, to wait and see. Mousseau whispered back for the interpreter to tell them we were looking for the downed chopper.

"Before the interpreter reached the NVA, our point man standing near the officer shouted out a command to us to search one part of the overgrown jungle area. We obeyed, realizing they thought he was in charge. Mousseau then whispered to me that he thought they saw my face and instructed me to take the guy out to the left the second out point man moved out of the way; he'd get the one on the right. All hell was about to break loose.

"But the NVA officer waved, apparently satisfied that we were all on the same side, as our point man, barking more orders, returned. We didn't know what to think at this time but we were ready. We thought we had fooled them but weren't certain.

"As the interpreter passed us, he whispered, '*They know.*' Mousseau, our point and I began raking them with automatic weapon fire. I had a Russian-made AK-47, Mousseau had an M-3 grease gun and the point liked a Sten.

"Our situation was no longer a secret, especially after one of the NVA who had been hit fired his RPG (Rocket-Propelled Grenade) that swooshed past our heads and burst in the trees, making a noise that rocked the jungle around us. We had cut down 10 of them, but one or two of the wounded tried to make it to safety. The rest of our Special Forces team cut them down with murderous automatic weapon fire.

"Leroy set up a woodline perimeter and planned to call for extraction. Our position *was* compromised now, no doubt about it! The TL immediately took out the plastic pouch from his shirt and removed a few documents from it, he told me to destroy them, quickly. He replaced the pouch in his shirt as Mousseau and I ignited a chunk of C-4 (plastic explosive we could shave that was excellent fuel for a fire), and we burned the documents.

"We were at the LZ waiting for the extraction slicks. We could hear their noisy engines not far away, accompanied by the chattering of small arms and machine gun fire. On silent insertions, they simply flew their zig-zag path in, dropped us in a few seconds and went away - fast. On a hot extraction, the helicopter gunships came in with the pickup choppers, doorgunners raking the treeline in all directions, the rockets and machine gun fire cutting a path and forcing the enemy to retreat into the safety of the jungle, thereby giving us a few added precious seconds to board the extraction slick to safety.

"There was a momentary break in the firing around us; it seemed everyone on the ground was firing at the approaching choppers. Wright called the FAC to reconfirm our exact location as the point of insertion. The team split in two groups to prepare for extraction.

"A single slick appeared but instead of hovering over the PZ, the pickup zone, it stayed at the far end, maybe 100 meters from us. As it was coming in, about five or six of the enemy approached it, waving it in. *God, they think they're us!*

"The CIDG began firing at the NVA as they walked into the open to signal the chopper. Then, the chopper doorgunner strafed *our* perimeter. We darted for cover while Wright tried to contact the FAC to tell them what was happening. Mousseau and I began to pick off a few of the NVA. At the same time, the doorgunner snapped to the scene and lowered his M-60, *blasting* the remaining NVA with a hail of 7.62mm death pellets.

"Wright told Mousseau to try and contact the chopper pilot with mirrors. If they didn't respond in seconds, he was to throw red and green flares on the PZ to alert the pilot where we were. I was trying to make radio contact with anyone who could hear me. Wright stood up behind a tree to get antenna height and I was able to reach the FAC to get the chopper in the air.

"Twenty or thirty NVA were advancing from the treeline across from us, heading toward the chopper. Wright told me to bring the LAW (light anti-tank weapon) to Mousseau to scatter those troops. Wright and I laid down grenade fire as more NVA broke from the woodline to rush the chopper. The slick gained altitude while both doorgunners raked devastating fire on the approaching enemy. Those M-60 machine guns spit out instant death as they chattered endlessly. The NVA were caught in a murderous crossfire between the doorgunners and us. The chopper gained altitude and left. We didn't take any casualties.

"Our team regrouped again further in the treeline on our side of the PZ and planned our next move for a successful extraction. Two of our CIDG's said they heard heavy vehicle movement coming toward us. Wright radioed the FAC to see what they could tell us.

"The enemy was close enough to us now for us to hear them shout orders to their troops. Wright told Mousseau and his team to secure a section of trees centered but towards our end of the PZ while we gave covering fire. Once they were settled, they could give cover fire for us as we made a mad dash for another tree stand and ant hill, leaving about 15 meters between for a chopper to land while we gave flank support.

"Mousseau's team reached its point without casualties. On our run, we passed his team on the route to ours. As we reached the tree and mound, the jungle exploded with automatic weapon fire and crew-operated weapons. We were caught.

"The team leader spun backwards, hitting me with his body and flailing arms. As I fell, I caught a round in the left arm. The TL recovered and yelled, *'get to the hill.'* Before reaching the hill, his body bounced and jerked in front of me. He fell, telling me he couldn't move his legs. Only God knows how four of us reached the ant hill. Looking back I saw two of our dead CIDG still being fired on, their bodies jerking and bumping as each burst hit them.

"Wright was on the radio while the rest of us laid down fire toward the grassy field where the NVA, supported by at least two crew-operated weapons, were firing. We heard Mousseau yell that he was hit as eight or ten NVA broke from the woodline and charged Mousseau's position.

"The interpreter began hurling grenades into the heavy auto to give Mousseau's team a chance to reorganize their cover as the team leader, a CIDG, and I laid down more fire to ease our problem.

"The heavy fire from the enemy lasted maybe two or three minutes. Gunships arrived on the scene as Wright signaled them to the two main points of enemy concentration. I looked up and saw more NVA running in the open field but, by now, Mousseau's team was in a better position to protect themselves from the woodbine fire.

"Small arms fire and RPG rounds began whistling down on us, and five NVA came running at us in a death charge. We took them down. Apparently one was only wounded and he was able to gently roll two grenades into our position. Wright threw the first grenade back and it exploded in the air. He yelled to us, *'get down, get down'* and laid his body on his side to protect us from the second grenade, the one he didn't have time to throw back.

"The explosion rocked his body and seemed to throw his legs in the air. I crawled to our heroic team leader. His head turned to me and he asked me to give him a gun. I couldn't believe he was still alive! Before we could get the radio or pass a rifle to him, a rifle grenade came over our heads and Mousseau yelled for us to lay down. As it exploded, Mousseau and the remaining CIDG opened full auto over our heads and killed the wounded NVA who fired the grenade. Mousseau then grabbed a LAW from one of the dead CIDG's and headed back to his position.

"Our CIDG handed Wright a rifle as I cut the strap on the TL's radio. The fire suddenly became so intense I had to hug the ground and settle for the hand-set from his radio. While the TL, interpreter, and CIDG laid down fire, I called the C & C. The traffic over the airwaves was heavy and the Command and Control chopper heard me and shut all other transmissions off to hear what I had to say.

"I do recall screaming and cursing; proper radio procedure would have to wait until a later time. The FAC told me about a downed chopper but that help was on the way. At this time, our team leader, Leroy Wright, the one who shielded us from that second grenade, took a round in the forehead. His head bobbed up and he settled to the ground, *dead*.

"I called for TAC (Tactical Air Command) *fast*. I was told it was less than two minutes away and they asked for target identification. Before I could respond, I took a hit in my left ankle and another in my right thigh.

"The FAC identified north and south for me and I was able to give the instructions he asked for. I was not able to tell him of the second team's position. He informed me he was in contact with Mousseau, that he was coming in, to mark the targets for the air strike and to keep on the frequency. I Rogered out.

"My interpreter had taken a machinegun burst in his arm. It was hanging on to the shoulder by muscle and skin. He tugged at me to say Mousseau wanted me. Firing and rolling on my side, I saw the ATL at his emergency radio. He called for ammo and grenades.

"I stripped two dead CIDG of their ammo and grenades and moved a meter or two and threw the clips and grenades to a CIDG who, in turn, threw them to Mousseau. The ATL pointed up then put his hand flat, knuckles up. I knew what he meant; hug the ground.

"The FAC was coming in with smoke. He asked 'on target' and I Rogered. He told us to lay low, the TAC would be coming in - close. They did come in, close too. They saturated the entire end of our side of the LZ with devastating firepower. The FAC asked something like, 'how's that?' I answered something like 'beautiful' or 'thanks.'

"We had a few minutes to patch up our wounds. I gave the interpreter a syrette of morphine and tied his arm with a tourniquet. I was able to clog a few leaks on my own body and gave myself a morphine hit. I ran an IV of albumin in my arm because of blood loss. Mousseau was doing the same. The CIDG was dressing his facial wound and wrapping his arm.

"The FAC was back on the air asking for more targets which I was able to give to him. Mousseau, propped against a couple of his dead CIDG's, pointed skyward with his radio in his hand. In came more TAC. Their sweeps were farther our from the PZ and their strikes shorter in duration. I reasoned they were short on ordnance and they were soon going to leave us.

"They came in one more time, screaming over the treetops, but the NVA were coming too. Mortar rounds, heavy automatic weapon fire, rockets and grenades filled the PZ. I caught a burst in the abdomen from an automatic weapon, and the radio was shot out. I was out of it and just laid behind the TL's body, firing at the NVA in the open field until the ammo ran out.

"The NVA fire was getting heavier as the sound of approaching choppers got closer. I was hoping it was the strike force coming in *en masse* to help us. But one lone slick appeared in the middle of the LZ and hovered ten or so feet off the ground with doorgunners blazing.

"A rucksack or pack of some kind came flying out followed by a USSF person who jumped to the ground, made a PLF (standard paratrooper landing fall), got to his feet, picked up the sack, and started running toward Mousseau's location. The slick took off right over my position and a web belt of ammo dropped but it landed beyond us in the trees.

"I watched as the SF trooper made a 75 to 100 yard dash toward me, falling down then getting up to run, and roll, and fall again. It was Staff Sergeant Benavidez. I couldn't believe it! What was happening? What in the *world* was he doing here?

"Benavidez reached Mousseau's team and immediately began giving them first-aid and repositioning them to include our area of the PZ. He got on the emergency radio and caught a glimpse of us and gestured 'thumbs up.' I replied with a head movement and poked the semiconscious interpreter to tell him about the sergeant's arrival.

"'*Don't leave me here,*' he begged. I assured him I

wouldn't. Benavidez yelled over. '*Connors, you okay?*' He gave him a 'thumbs up' and I shouted back '*ammo*.' He said okay and asked who was alive? I raised two fingers saying 'me and the interpreter.'

"Benavidez told us to try and get over to his position and said we were '*going out*'. The interpreter and I tried to get over to him as a slick was making raking passes overhead and light automatic weapon fire opened up and pinned us down. Benavidez waved us back and threw smoke.

"The slick came in and Benavidez began loading Mousseau and the wounded CIDG. The chopper moved toward our location with Benavidez running alongside firing his weapon, one he apparently picked up along the way. He dove in next to me and asked if we could walk. I told him I could crawl but the interpreter was now unconscious. He asked about Leroy and whether he had the SOI papers still on him. I told him we had burned *some* of the papers. I didn't know about all of them. I mentioned the plastic pouch in the dead team leader's shirt and about radio frequencies that were possibly still in the pouch. I think Roy had three or four bullet wounds in him at this time. I'd seen him take two hits. It didn't seem to bother him.

"Seeing all I had was a .22 pistol left with ammo, he handed me his rifle and said to cover him. As I covered him, Benavidez went to the interpreter to get his grenades and immediately pulled the pins and threw them in the tall grass beyond the TL. Two NVA popped up and started to run, but the blasts from Roy's grenades shuttled them both skyward.

"Benavidez pushed the interpreter and made him crawl to my position then took his weapon back and shouted to us to crawl to the chopper because we were too close to the trees. The last I recall was me and the interpreter crawling on our hands and knees toward the chopper, I looked up to see a CIDG grab for me - then some kind of explosion and everything went black."

Viet Cong or friendlies? You could never really tell.

Men, women and children fought for the North and South.

THE FORWARD AIR CONTROLLER

The forward air controller (FAC) is the name given the pilot of a small aircraft who flies over the jungle giving reports on troop movements, firefights, or directs artillery, anything he feels would be helpful to the command post. This airplane, with the FAC at the controls, flies back and forth, seemingly willy-nilly, looking, reporting or directing.

On special missions there is always a Command and Control helicopter hovering at about 5000 feet above directing the insertion and extraction choppers on the proper vectors. This C & C chopper is in direct radio contact with the ground forces and, in turn, talks to the FAC who is usually buzzing over and around the area of insertion to direct the assault aircraft to the target. There is no need for the FAC to be too concerned over giving away the team's position since it has already been compromised.

I was fortunate enough to be given a letter written to Roy concerning the events this particular day by the FAC who was flying that mission on May 2nd, 1968. He was fresh out of the United States Air Force military academy at that time, and a second lieutenant. When he wrote the letter on November 28, 1988 he was a colonel. Now, in 1990 he is a Brigadier General in the USAF. His name is Robin M. Tornow and he is presently stationed somewhere in Panama.

THE LETTER:

"Over the years, I have recalled the events of that fateful day in May of 1968. I'm sure that time has warped some of the detail, but I think I can present another perspective that will add to the events of that day.

"We launched a mid-morning insertion out of Loc Ninh. This was not a standard 6-man package, but a 12-man reinforced team whose purpose was to gain proof that vehicles were traveling through Cambodia into Viet Nam. The team was to capture a truck if feasible.

"The insertion was made right on the border between Cambodia and Viet Nam about 15 miles southwest of Loc Ninh. Following the insertion, the support and communications team set up a base camp at Loc Ninh. [This was where Roy was stationed and heard the radio blaring after the team had been met with heavy fire].

"We put 5 UH-1 slicks and 5 UH-1 gunships in there as well so we could respond quickly if the team got in trouble. I circled in the area, maintaining radio contact with the team from my O-1F Bird Dog (small single-engine aircraft). As the FAC, I would make certain that the team was inserted at the right place and then I'd stay around for about an hour until the team felt secure and that it had not been seen by enemy forces.

"About 30-minutes after insertion, the team called me to say they had been spotted and their position was compromised. The best policy was to pull a team out as soon as they were seen. In this case, however, the Detachment Commander, Colonel Ralph Drake, receiving orders from the higher command, made the decision to keep the team in. He had me relay to the team that they should evade and stay concealed until the threat passed and then continue with their mission.

"The team acknowledged and all appeared okay. After another 30-minutes, an Army Bird Dog (Seahorse was his call sign) came on station to provide radio relay. I briefed him on the situation and then returned to Loc Ninh to sit alert.

"All remained quiet for nearly an hour. Suddenly we received a call from the radio relay that our forces were receiving fire. Everyone knew this meant we were going in for extraction.

"Gunships, slicks, and FAC all scrambled and took off. As soon as I was airborne, I came up on frequency with the team and knew immediately that they were in deep trouble. The radio operator was desperate. He'd been hit more times than he could remember and an explosion had left him blinded. He knew some of the team was already dead. Everyone still alive was fighting for his life. The fighting was fierce.

"As I approached the target area, I heard the gunships call that they were picking up intense fire. One of them called that he had taken hits in his engine and was turning back. Shortly thereafter he made a controlled crash into the trees about a mile from the hot zone. Immediately, the remaining slicks pulled back and concentrated their efforts on rescuing the downed chopper crew.

"I concentrated my effort on the team. Everywhere I looked, I saw swarming khaki uniforms. I estimated nearly 250 NVA in the open. No telling how many were still in the trees. It was obvious that we'd fallen into a main NVA base camp.

"In an impulsive reaction, I tuned my radio to the international emergency frequency and called, 'Mayday, Mayday, Mayday.' I called for any fighters in the area. I needed anything I could get. 'Vector 10 miles southwest of Loc Ninh. I need to put you in immediately. Troops in heavy contact.'

"Within 5-minutes I had 2, F-100's respond. These guys were pros and understood what they needed to do. Napalm, CBU-29, and strafe was their load.

"The napalm was gone in two passes. It took out most of the swarm in the open and pressure off our troops. The remainder of the NVA ran for the safety and cover of the trees. Next the pilots put in the CBU (cluster bomb unit). This was not the standard Cluster Bomb Unit; this stuff was variable delay fusing.

"The fighters rolled in, screaming over the treetops and released their cluster bombs. Nothing happened! I asked the fighters what went wrong? *'Just wait a few minutes,'* they replied.

"Before their words faded from their answer, the CBU started exploding, just like popcorn. This kept on for more than two hours and really forced the NVA to pull back and take cover. They couldn't figure it out. Just about then, the fighters rolled in again with their guns, working the treeline against the most persistent enemy gunners.

"Following two more sets of fighters and helicopter gunships adding firepower for those on the ground, we were ready to try the extraction again. As the gunships continued to circle with suppressive fire, we put the lead slick into the LZ nearest our troops (McKibben's chopper). The first mission was to pull out the alive and wounded. We'd come in for the dead later."

And the battle raged. Benavidez and O'Connor had no idea what the plan was. They were fighting for their lives. Mortar rounds, automatic weapon fire, and grenades were coming in on them from the enemy. Air support had napalm and CBU units from the fighters, rockets and Gatling guns from the helicopter gunships and, of course, the ever-present doorgunners raking the treeline with their M-60's, but the enemy had them surrounded. Benavidez guessed at 300 or more of the NVA. From Tornows position as FAC it could have been 500; he reported over 250 in the open.

It isn't clear if the FAC heard O'Connor or Roy over his radio, but it seems it was Roy's voice. Roy had shards of sharp metal from the mortar rounds lodged in his face, neck, and head. The blood from these wounds blinded Roy and the young lieutenant in that small aircraft reported that the radio operator was blinded.

"The task was difficult because the wounded were unable to move, pinned down by continuous enemy fire," Colonel Tornow wrote. "The recovery crew on the slick fanned out to drag as many as possible to the helicopter. After what seemed like an eternity, the helicopter began to lift off.

"As the chopper began to lift, an enemy soldier stepped out and unloaded his AK-47 on the pilot. It was Warrant Officer Larry McKibben. Almost in slow motion the helicopter spun awkwardly, the blades slicing into the trees, and in a moment lay in a twisted shambles on the ground. All motion ceased, and I was faced with the despair of now having 17 people on the ground.

"For the next two hours we continued to put in gunships and fighters until our reinforcement company could be inserted to secure the area. Throughout this period, the remaining troops on the ground held out against impossible odds.

"Three hours after the fight began, we completed extraction of these 17 courageous fighters. In all, 9 of the 17 were brought out alive - an amazing feat to say the least.

"My 6-months as a FAC with B-56 were probably *the* most fulfilling in my career. I'll always reflect proudly on having served with such a great group of dedicated professionals. It was my distinct honor to meet you again this past summer [he's addressing Roy]. I wish you continued success in your life and I salute you as a great American."

* My latest report confirmed listed but *three* of those wounded that day survived the mission.

After bombs, napalm, rockets, and machinegun fire, there was little left of trees or vegetation.

SIX HOURS IN HELL

Roy had taken three, maybe four hits. He didn't know if he could walk, but he'd try. He doesn't recall thinking of anything at this time, every move was automatic. He had been trained well as a Green Beret. He knew he'd have to call on the impossible now but he was ready to try.

"*Try to get to the slick*," Roy told O'Connor. "*I'm going after the papers and Leroy.*" The last Roy saw of O'Connor was him and the wounded CIDG crawling toward the extraction chopper.

With agonizing pain Roy rose to his feet. He took one step forward and he didn't fall. He tried to put pain out of his mind. He had a mission and that was all that mattered. He took another step and another and he was still on his feet. He was moving forward to find Leroy and the SOI papers. Roy made it to the team leader's body. Crouching beside him, Roy reached inside Leroy's shirt to retrieve the plastic pouch. As he looked at his dead friend, he removed his hand from the shirt. "*I won't leave you here, Leroy. You deserve better than that.*" He knew if he left him, the NVA might string the body to a tree and maybe gut him to show other Americans what would happen to them. No, Roy would not leave Leroy to that.

Roy reached under Leroy's arms to heft him onto his shoulders so he could carry him to McKibben's extraction chopper. He left the papers, camera, and radio on Leroy, planning to carry them with Leroy's body to the extraction slick. That was when he took his big hit, the round from the AK-47 that entered his back on the lower right side and exited under his left armpit, turning, twisting, tearing, and leaving particles near - even *in* - his heart. He was leaning over trying to get Wright to his shoulders, his left arm extended, when he took that hit. Had he not been lifting the team leader, chances are the round would have gone through his left arm also.

Roy dropped Leroy and fell forward on his face. Just before he blacked out, he recalls hearing a loud, nearby explosion. "*The slick,*" he thought. "*The slick's been hit.*" Then...the lights went out.

When Roy awoke he had, momentarily, forgotten where he was. The pain quickly snapped his memory back to reality. He tried to move but the hurt was so intense he screamed. He lifted his head to see what was happening. He didn't know how long he had been unconscious.

"It was difficult to breathe," he told me. "I knew I was hurt bad and my entire upper body was soaked in blood. As I surveyed the gaping hole under my left arm, I almost blacked out again. But I think I stayed awake because the pain was so terrible. I knew I had to get up - *now* - or stay there forever. The chopper was landing and I saw O'Connor and the CIDG crawling toward it. Yeah, I can make it to the chopper and drag Leroy along with me."

But the chopper was not there. It was farther up the LZ, at the edge of the treeline and smoking - a mangled mess of steel. Men were crawling from the wreckage. The explosion he heard was the sound of the chopper slamming into the ground.

"I limped to the wreckage, not too very far from where I was last hit. The NVA were across from us laying down withering fire trying to finish off the crew.

"I saw McKibben through the cockpit window. He was slumped over in his seat, still strapped in, and covered with blood. Chopper parts were scattered everywhere. The 2000-pound transmission had crushed one of the doorgunners and was lying grotesquely on his chest. His eyes were almost popping from his face because of the tremendous weight.

"The co-pilot, Fernan, had the branch of a tree about the size of a fat pencil stuck in his left ear. Blood covered his neck and was running down his arm and chest. He came around from the back of the slick waving his .38 in the air. When McKibben was shot, the chopper went out of control. It crashed then darted forward, the limb catching Fernan as the craft slammed into the treeline."

Roy was coughing as he tried to speak, spitting up blood. But cries from inside the slick snapped him from his momentary thoughts. He shuffled to the door to help what seemed to be the last man out of the chopper. That was when he saw O'Connor lying on his back in the grass, the interpreter next to him. "Guess they never made it to the chopper," Roy thought.

A CIDG who was the least of the wounded was right at Roy's feet. Roy pulled him up and told him to get the radio from O'Connor. By gesturing to his head and mouth, Roy was able to convey his message. As he reached the wounded radioman calling *"Connors, Connors,"* O'Connor rolled over and looked at Benavidez. *"You still alive, Big Team?"* Roy asked, shocked that O'Connor was still alive. *"I think so,"* came the reply.

"Mousseau, one of McKibben's doorgunners, and three CIDG had made their way to the broken tail section of the chopper and were returning fire from the enemy. I didn't even think of the fire. I don't know what I thought.

"The smell of fuel was everywhere. You can never forget the stench of JP-4. I knew the chopper was going to blow in seconds. One CIDG yelled 'ammo' and wanted to get it from the chopper. I ordered him to join O'Connor and get guns and ammo from the dead. Mousseau and his men began crawling to cover in another stand of trees."

Roy reached Mousseau and his group who had clustered

together around three trees, surrounded by Elephant grass. They were about 40 feet from O'Connor and the others.

The NVA were raining mortar rounds on the downed helicopter and shards of metal were shooting in all directions. Roy felt his face sting but was able to ignore any reaction. When the mortar fire lessened, Roy took the radio he had borrowed from O'Connor and tried to call the FAC. He couldn't *see* and tried to clear his eyes. His head was covered with blood. As he tried to wipe the blood, he cut his hands on the shards of metal sticking from his head, neck, and face. He hadn't even felt the pain.

Few, if any, combat veterans recall ever thinking when they are in the heat of battle. Roy, however, had various respites in battle, you know, moments here and there when there was a lull in the shooting. He told me he had one flashing thought about that time when he was a kid in Cuero, Texas and he saw that sign on the restaurant door stating, "*Mexicans and dogs not allowed. Niggers use the back door.*" He said he wished that restaurant owner was there now to see him. He would have been proud. But Roy had other things to think about, like getting out of that mess.

"*For God's sake*," Roy called over the radio, "*bring in some air support!*" The FAC asked for target coordinates and Roy called for close strikes. Most of the team were dead or wounded and surrounded by NVA who were getting closer with each passing second. Sure, Roy wanted to live but if he died, he'd prefer getting it from his own who were trying to save him and his comrades, not the NVA.

And in they came. Within minutes the F-100's began dropping their loads, firing rockets and Gatling guns. Helicopter gunships appeared from nowhere and were knocking down trees and brush with their machine gun fire. Napalm hit and scattered bodies and undergrowth in all directions and the fire burned so close, it scorched O'Connor's face. Roy was calling it in close, for certain. And those crackerjack Air Force flyboys did their job. One report had it that there were over 20 of the F-4's, fully armed and waiting to swoop down in one-minute intervals. A helicopter pilot who was at the scene said, "The trees, brush, even the ground was on fire," he told me. "And I heard that tough, little Mexican down there calling off coordinates and throwing smoke and saying he was wiping blood from his eyes. It was a raging battle going on. I had the catbird seat and I could see it all."

As the enemy retreated farther in the trees, Roy began patching up wounded and giving them shots of morphine. He gave himself two syrettes of morphine too. He was still awake - wide awake. Mousseau and one of the CIDG's were in bad shape. Mousseau was only semi-conscious from loss of blood. His eye was still hanging and he was covered with bandages and blood. The belly-wound in the CIDG was ripped wide, his intestines were poking out. Roy tried to put them back, placing the CIDG's hand over the wound. While Roy was bandaging him, he continued begging Roy to kill him. Roy thought about it for a brief moment then decided, in his own mind, that they were going to be rescued. It was only a matter of time.

In the meantime, the heavy firing started again ··· as the gunships and aircraft subsided. It was like a game; the gunships came in and strafed the treeline and the NVA retreated. When the air support left to rearm, the NVA came out again and began firing.

Roy took another hit. He wasn't certain where, but the force knocked him down again. He went flat, tears, blood, and sweat clotting his vision. He only felt a hard slap, no pain. The morphine must have been doing its job.

Benavidez moved toward O'Connor who must have seen him take the hit since he asked Roy if he was okay. Roy replied he wasn't certain. *"I been hit so much, I can't feel nothing anymore."*

"Save your ammo until you see somebody trying to get to us," Roy told O'Connor. Roy and a CIDG crawled forward to retrieve some NVA bodies and dragged them back to O'Connor to form a human barricade. As they tried to get another body, the firing from the woods came in like sheets of rain and Roy took another shot in his left leg while the CIDG screamed from a burst which hit him in the stomach. Roy dragged him to O'Connor where he noticed a piece of shrapnel had entered the radioman's body, just above the left kidney. Roy looked for the radio but couldn't find it. He shook O'Connor, asking for the radio and got a glimpse of it under O'Connor's body.

Roy called for more help and managed to point out where the last burst of fire had come from. In seconds, a rocket from somewhere *"up there"* erupted in a burst of fire, taking out the attackers.

O'Connor was still awake and told Roy he had a few syrettes of morphine in his back pocket. Roy gave O'Connor one and took the other himself. He rebandaged O'Connor's wounds, patched up the CIDG with the stomach wound, and tightened the tourniquet on the interpreter's arm.

Roy couldn't see or think too clearly and it was almost impossible for him to call in and direct any additional air strikes. The FAC called down and said they had them spotted, just hug the ground. *"We're coming in low and close."*

Benavidez asked O'Connor to cover him while he went after Mousseau. "I began crawling," Roy told me. "I was able to push with one leg, pull with my right arm and move forward toward Mousseau and his men. Bullets whizzed and hissed all around me as O'Connor and his wounded and dying comrades tried to return the fire. By some miracle I reached the trees where Mousseau and his men were in hiding.

"The Vietnamese with the stomach wound was still begging for someone to kill him. The NVA had us surrounded and were firing from everywhere. They weren't certain exactly where we were but they knew we were there and continued firing without letup.

"Men were crying and screaming. They were praying, cursing, begging the Lord for help. I was one of them. We were going to die. There was no doubt about it now.

"Suddenly, the sound of the jets overhead coming down in a death-dealing dive rose above it all. They came in low and close as promised, their afterburners scorching the treetops and the bombs falling and rockets roaring almost on top of us. We were showered with broken tree branches, dirt, hot metal, and burning debris. We loved it!

"In moments they were gone. Then the helicopter gunships moved in, circling us and spewing hot lead in the jungle below. One of them took a hit and headed for the trees near us. It was able to autorotate down but was smoking badly. The wounded crewmen began to crawl toward us and I shouted for them to take cover and stay away and not compromise our position.

"A radio message blurted through the haze. *'We're coming in to get you,'* the message squawked. *'How could we get out of here?'* I thought. The surrounding fire stopped, but I knew it would return in minutes, hardly enough time to get a slick in and get us out. But if they would try, so would I.

"In the momentary lull, the sound of one lone slick

pierced my ears. The chopper came from the heavens - no doubt - and whipped in through the smoke and landed right in the center of the PZ and settled to earth maybe twenty or thirty meters from us. Warrant Officer Roger Waggie was at the controls."

Chopper pilot Warrant Officer Roger Waggie flew over 1000 hours in combat and received 39 Air Medals.

ROGER WAGGIE

Roger had served one tour in Vietnam in 3rd Special Forces as a sergeant. He returned to the states and completed helicopter training and volunteered to go back to the Nam. He can't reason why, to this day he can't, other than he, like Roy, believed in what he was doing.

I got his telephone number and address from Roy and called him. We talked via telephone and visited by several letters. In fact, Roger is in the process of writing his own book and, I promise, it will be as unbelievable as any you've ever read. Roger is quite a guy; let me tell you some things about him.

He flew over a *thousand* combat hours while serving in Vietnam, yet Roger has only been wounded on one occasion when his chopper was shot down on March 4th, 1968 near Dong Tam. He was hit in the legs, chest, and a piece of shrapnel went through his cheek - in one side and out the other - and missed everything in between. Roger mentions it matter-of-factly.

In visiting with a comrade of his who flew with Roger, he told me of the time when bullets came zinging into the chopper and Roger took a few rounds that banged into his chest plate. Roger looked down, slid his chest plate aside, and picked one round from sticking inside his chest, half in and half out of the skin. "*Looks like rivets are coming out of this thing*," he joked, as he took a few of the flattened bullets that had torn his clothing but stopped at the plate. He then threw them casually on the floor, and gave himself first aid for the slug he plucked from his chest. He didn't report the incident. The fact that he wasn't wounded that day of May 2nd puzzles him. "There was enough of 'em down there... looked like 300 or so, and they were throwing everything they had at us. My chopper had so many holes in it they scrapped it after that day."

For several months he flew but couldn't recall a day of any of it. Only after his time in the VA Hospital in Salem, Virginia, and being hypnotized, was he able to recall what went on. He has no idea how many extractions he conducted during those months.

Roger is a hillbilly and proud of it. He is also the type of guy who will help anyone who needs it. In reality, he is afraid of nothing. He either feels he can never be hurt or just doesn't worry about it. Yes, a special guy, a natural hero-type. Let me share with you some of what he told me during our conversations.

Waggie, the way I understand it, landed at Loc Ninh that morning of May 2nd, with Craig, his wounded door gunner. After his chopper had a quick once-over to access the damage, he was in the air again, many instruments shot out. He considered his aircraft questionable for flight but he was a combat veteran; a green chopper pilot would not have flown. When he heard Roy and O'Connor over his radio he knew they were in trouble and needed help - *fast*. Immediately, he headed for Cambodia and the hot zone where Roy and the other Green Berets were trapped. Warrant Officer Dave Hoffman was his co-pilot, but he was short a crew chief and a door gunner. The enlisted men manning those positions had been killed and two Warrant Officers, Bill Darling and Tom Smith, volunteered to act as replacements. A Special Forces medic, Staff Sergeant Sammons, also volunteered to make the trip. They all knew they were flying into hell.

"I had 47 holes in my chopper from that first run when Craig got hit, one hole in the tail rotor drive cover was as big as a softball. And I didn't just 'happen' to be in the area, this was a bonafide *Sigma* operation. Roy didn't know it at the time, but the mission was to steal a Russian truck from the Ho Chi Minh Trail to show the world that Cambodia was not neutral, that troops and supplies were coming in through Cambodia and yet we weren't allowed in because it was '*neutral.*' When I heard Roy and Brian over the radio, I knew they had but minutes to live and couldn't wait for other help. My volunteer crew and I knew our chances of survival were slim but we did it anyway."

As Waggie approached the hot zone, he did what he had done countless times before; he bore in and landed, door gunners strafing the treeline, Smith on one gun and Darling on the gun behind Waggie.

Warrant Officer Bill Darling wrote. "After we got airborne, I switched the radio channel to the Special Forces team only to hear SSG Benavidez giving directions and taking charge of the situation. It seems that WO McKibben had been shot and killed and his aircraft was down in the LZ. We were next to go in, at treetop level. I could see all the gunships getting it the worst and saw McKibben's chopper turned almost upside down - smoking, and propped against a tree. I could see McKibben still strapped in and blood covering his face.

"We landed within ten meters of the downed aircraft, and the Special Forces team began running toward our chopper. I was on the machine gun putting out fire from the tail boom to as close as I could to the team.

"Loading was slow and it gave SSG Benavidez time to make *three trips* from the downed aircraft to our ship, carrying wounded. I saw him carrying radio equipment and a badly wounded interpreter under one arm. In fact, on one of his trips, he shot two of the enemy who were behind our helicopter and whom I couldn't get with my machine gun. On his final trip he was holding his intestines in his arms - I didn't think he would make it back; he was badly wounded."

What Warrant Officer Bill Darling didn't tell was how *many* of the enemy he spotted as they were about to land. Waggie said the area was crawling with NVA, maybe a hundred or so running and shooting, some on one knee and firing automatic weapons at the approaching chopper. It was like a shoot-out in one of those old Western movies, the NVA there and our guys coming right at them from above, guns blazing in each other's face.

As the chopper touched down that first time, the enemy was on the aircraft like ants on a pie. Waggie shot two of the NVA through his side window with his .38 as they rushed the helicopter from the front. They were clamoring on the aircraft trying to get in the doors. One NVA tried to bayonet Hoffman through the windshield.

Smith and Darling were laying down withering fire, shooting at the mass of bodies running toward them, as the NVA who were near the aircraft were yelling, shooting, swinging their arms and trying to get inside at the Americans.

Waggie took the chopper airborne again, up to about 200 feet, and shook the NVA off who were hanging on the skids and doors. Once he got thumbs up from his door gunners, he circled and came in for another try at a landing.

Benavidez told me that Darling was laying down fire from his M-60 machine gun that kept most of the NVA in the woods. But when he came back to the chopper, holding his side to keep his guts from coming out, Darling got off the gun to help him. This was when Darling took a hit in the shoulder and was thrown back into the chopper. Darling still managed to separate the dead from the wounded and give whatever first-aid he could to those who were still alive.

Warrant Officers Darling and Smith *volunteered* for this mission even though they all knew the odds were against them. Perhaps they didn't think about the odds either and it too was *Involuntary Reflex Action*, as Roy describes his reason for going in. These men were all heroes.

I haven't any information on the medals they were awarded but Waggie, for instance, has an Air Medal with *thirty-eight* Oak Leaf Clusters (one cluster for each award). While going through files, veteran CO's think it's a typographical error. But why not a Silver Star or DSC? And for Darling, volunteering, wounded and still firing, tending the wounded, risking his life against almost impossible odds, why *not* a Medal of Honor for him? His heroic act that day fulfills all the criteria. He didn't even get a Purple Heart that day. By his own choosing *he* tended his shoulder wound and never reported it. Perhaps there was so much sacrifice, so much heroism going on, that these men and their feats were overlooked. Or perhaps their commanding officer wasn't aware of the magnitude of their valor, or neglected to mention it in his report?

But Roy Benavidez knows their worth. If not for them, for Waggie and Hoffman, for Smith and Sammons, and certainly Bill Darling, he might not be with us today, and he mentions each of them in his prayers every night. I've heard him pray.

When Waggie first landed, he saw "*about a hundred NVA coming from the woods.*" He saw the huddled band of his comrades trying to make it to his chopper and he went back in on his second attempt, door gunners blasting from all directions. The chopper touched down, and did a dance in the grass as the skids settled. Sergeant Sammons leaped from the extraction slick to begin loading the wounded. Waggie recalls seeing Roy, limping, bleeding, covered with blood, carrying wounded and tossing them in the chopper then going back for more, falling, getting up, and dragging bodies back to the extraction slick, then going in again.

"Once everyone was loaded, I applied power and the engine strained from the additional weight. My payload is right at 11 and I had at least 17 on board. The piles were stacked quickly; dead in one pile and wounded in the other. I saw Sammons and Darling pulling Benavidez aboard and I saw Darling take the hits. If Benavidez had made one more trip, I'd have left him. Bullets were thudding and thunking in the sides of my chopper and I wasn't sure if any of us would make it. Maximum time to set is maybe 10 seconds. I was down maybe three minutes - or four. The Lord really was on our side, there can be no other explanation.

"My turbines whined and the engine strained during the takeoff; the nose was down and blood from the dead and wounded was flowing so freely it washed around my feet. When I leveled off, it ran from the cargo doors like two faucets were turned on. Once we were airborne, my warning panel looked like a Christmas tree. All I had to go by was a magnetic compass and I was flying further into Cambodia, in shock, I'm certain. I glanced back at Mousseau and all I could see was his eyeball hanging down on his face and blood covering him."

Darling added, "we started giving first-aid to the wounded which meant little more than putting the live people on top of the dead. SSG Benavidez was at the front of the aircraft - I don't believe he received any attention because bodies were piled high and we couldn't get to many of them."

For Waggie, this was but one day in May. He did the same thing countless times for eight months. "Many times," he told me, "I wondered why I hadn't been hit that day but fortunately for Roy and the others, I wasn't. I've been lucky."

Yeah, lucky for certain, and just plain wild. Waggie must have coffee when he first gets up in the morning or he's a bit grumpy. A story told to me by one of his door gunners was about the morning Waggie and his crew were heating coffee in a canteen cup, using shavings of C-4 as fuel. A nearby sniper, perched high in a tree, began taking potshots at them. This was common, and you just got used to it, but the sniper started coming close and a few bullets knocked up dirt on Waggie's boots, ones he had just shined. Usually, if the bullets came close, you'd just move out of the line of fire and forget about it, and let the SF guys get him later on in the day. But Waggie was grumpy; he hadn't had his first cup of coffee. "*Com'on*," he said to his door gunner, SP-4 Delarno, "*let's go hose him*." They got in the chopper, circled the camp, and Delarno shot the sniper out of the tree. They landed, went back to their coffee, and continued the conversation where they had left off.

But the war took its toll on Waggie's feelings. After picking up Roy and that crew from Cambodia, Waggie landed his chopper in the center of the airstrip at Quon Loi, and walked away. He didn't want to see what had happened that day. He and fellow-pilot Jerry Ewing went back to their tents and cried over it all, especially about their close friend and comrade, Warrant Officer Larry McKibben. A door gunner from Ewing's chopper went in and recovered McKibben's body. Waggie's chopper was so busted up that it was scrapped for parts and Waggie did a stint flying helicopter Gunships. He liked the fact that he now had the firepower to shoot back.

On June 8th, 1968, Waggie returned to find that his

other friends who were pilots, Dave Hoffman and Tom Smith, had been killed. The other pilot, Fernan, the co-pilot on McKibben's slick - the one with the piece of tree in his ear - was declared MIA, Missing In Action. In 1980 they declared him KIA, Killed In Action. Warrant Officer Jerry Ewing did not fly combat missions after that day in May.

But the war still hasn't ended for Warrant Officer/extraction chopper pilot/Special Forces hero Roger Waggie. He makes far too many visits to the VA Hospital in Salem, Virginia. His outside scars don't bother him as much as his inside scars. To this day he hurts inside and his memory won't allow him much peace.

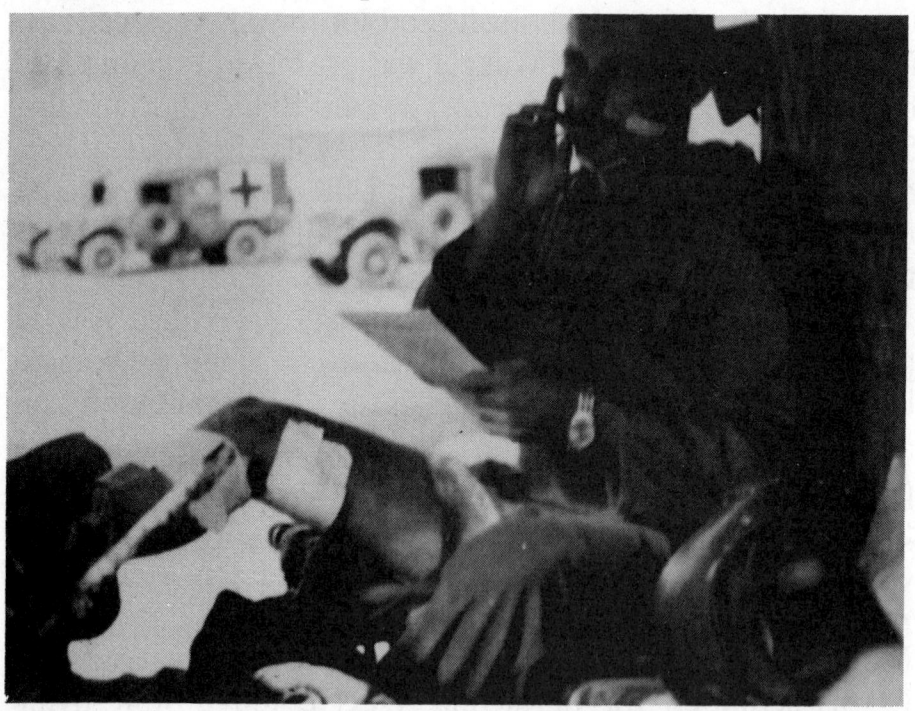

Waggie was shot down March 4th, 1968 and sprayed with shrapnel. He was also shot down March 8th and March 12th.

MANO A MANO

Roy saw Waggie's chopper coming in to touch down and immediately began to push and pull wounded toward the waiting aircraft. Special Forces Sergeant Sammons leaped to the ground and began giving first-aid while trying to load the wounded. Two of the men being helped aboard were slammed forward by enemy gunfire as they tried to board the slick. Warrant Officer Darling was on the side Roy could see and was sending a sizzling barrage of 7.62mm missiles of instant death at the advancing NVA.

Roy ran back, trying to find anyone he could to load, hoping they'd still be alive. Blood blotted most of his vision and his head was spinning. The wounds, even with the morphine and adrenalin and his indomitable will to survive, were beginning to take their toll on this Special Forces veteran. He watched the ground constantly and, luckily, found Mousseau lying in the grass. He summoned his last bit of energy and with a prayer to God, he was able to heft Mousseau to a shoulder and began to walk slowly, side-to--side, knees buckling now and then, falling, getting up and falling again, but forward to the safety of the chopper.

An NVA popped from the tall grass behind Roy, and Benavidez felt his head explode. He staggered forward, reeling, grenades going off inside his skull. He had been clubbed from behind by an NVA with the rifle butt of an AK-47!

Hadn't he taken enough? Was God against him? He prayed all through the six hours he had just spent in hell. He made the sign of the cross over and over again before he jumped from the helicopter and even more after he landed. He always believed in God and worshiped Him throughout his life. He felt that God was the reason he had survived so far. He gave God credit for everything good that happened to him and when good things didn't happen, he felt it was because He wanted to teach him something. Where was God now? He needed Him now - *badly*.

God answered! Roy *didn't* fall! He doesn't remember dropping Mousseau but found himself standing. Turning around, he was face-to-face with his attacker, who was pulling his rifle back and hesitating a moment, not believing that this Green Beret was still standing.

The NVA snarled and came forward, his bayonet swinging and catching Roy on the right arm, the blade stopping when it hit bone. The North Vietnamese Army regular pulled the bayonet back and came over with the rifle butt again, slamming Roy in the mouth, breaking teeth and snapping his jaw with the smash. *Still*...Roy didn't fall! *"Only God,"* Roy told me with a grim look on his face, *"could have prevented me from falling. If I had fallen, I'd have been killed."*

The enemy, apparently dumbfounded that the American was still on his feet, swung his rifle again, bayonet twirling and aiming for Roy's stomach. As he lunged, Roy sidestepped and caught the bayonet in the crook of his left forearm. The Green Beret clamped down and the NVA tried to pull the rifle back, the bayonet sawing into the flesh on Roy's arm. Back and forth, back and forth they went in a ghastly game of tug-a-war, the NVA trying to free his bayonet, and Roy, holding his arm tight to keep the bayonet from piercing his stomach.

Roy, from hours of training each day, reached to his side with his right hand and got a grip on the handle of his Bowie knife resting and waiting in its scabbard just below his beltline on his right hip.

"Involuntary reflex action again," Roy smiled, *"or maybe it was instinct. I think it was my Special Forces training of survival, but whatever it was, I did it."* And Roy did do it.

He was screaming from the top of his lungs, and he was spitting and crying as he wrapped his fingers around that handle and pulled the knife from its sheath. With all the strength he could muster, he plunged the 9 1/2 inches of sharp steel into his attacker. He took the knife out and dug it in again, twisting, it still screaming like a madman.

When he felt the life ebb from his adversary, he finished by slamming his foe to the ground, his chewed up left forearm jammed under the NVA's chin, the knife wedged between meat and bone. *"Then, I followed him to the blood soaked grass, trying to push his head through the planet."*

"I do recall getting a glimpse of O'Connor only a few feet away and I yelled to him to shoot the NVA when I first clamped my left arm around the bayonet. O'Connor was so busted up and so out of it with the morphine and actual exhaustion, I don't think he heard me.

Roy tried to get his knife back, but it was lodged tight and he was too weak to make but one feeble try. He recalls getting to his feet and seeing the chopper still waiting. He had no idea how long it was there or how long the actual fight lasted, maybe a minute, two at the most. It seemed like a lifetime.

It had been a mystery to Roy as to why the NVA didn't just *shoot* him, the same as Indiana Jones did in that adventure movie, *Raiders of the Lost Ark*; when the big sword-weilding ruffian came at Ford. The facts, as was learned later, was the NVA wanted to *try* for a prisoner. When the two hard hits with his weapon didn't fell Roy, he had to then fight for his life and forget about taking Roy alive, apparently forgetting that his weapon could, in fact shoot. Who knows what happens in these life-and-death situations. Whatever the reason, Roy is certainly thankful.

As Roy moved forward, he tripped over Mousseau lying

unconscious in the grass. In a last attempt to get Mousseau to the chopper he was able to muster enough strength to lift him, at the same time grabbing the dead NVA's AK-47.

Approaching the chopper, Mousseau on one shoulder, blood and sweat blocking out most of his vision, he saw two NVA coming from the rear, apparently out of vision of the door gunners. Roy raised his borrowed AK-47 and shot them both. He loaded Mousseau and went back to help the medic with O'Connor. O'Connor left a blood-trail in the grass as Roy and Sammons were dragging him to the chopper. He was awake enough to ask somebody to get his interpreter as arms reached down to pull him into the helicopter. Sammons went off in one direction and Roy went to search for the interpreter.

Roy, still moving and at war, ran, fell, tripped, got up again and ran some more, head down, firing in the brush before him with the AK-47 to avoid any other hidden *surprises*. He followed the blood-trail left by O'Connor and within seconds, he found the interpreter. He knew time was getting short with the helicopter; it was taking a terrific pounding.

Unbelievably, the brave sergeant lifted the interpreter onto his shoulder and made it back to the helicopter. Leroy Wright's body, with the pouch and camera, was already on the chopper. Then, Roy made one more trip to get wounded! This was when he, mistakenly, loaded three dead NVA, thinking they were his CIDG comrades.

With eyes almost closed from drying blood, with not an ounce of strength left in his tired, tortured, and bullet-ridden body, Roy was pulled aboard the safety of the slick by Sammons and Darling, the AK-47, on semi-automatic, still barking as Roy moved his finger on the trigger, raking the disappearing treeline.

This is "the" slick that recovered Roy and others on May 2nd. It was scrapped after that mission with over 200 holes in it.

Warrant Officer Roche, KIA June, 1968; Waggie; W/O Addison, KIA June of '68; W/O Bill Darling, WIA May 2nd and August of 1968.

"Frenchy" Mousseau and W/O Hoffman, co-pilot on Waggie's extraction slick.

Fussell, Waggie, McKibben, Naul and Armstrong (kneeling).

Special Forces on patrol. Some study maps while others watch for the enemy.

Perfect camouflage - blend in with your surroundings and - don't move.

Rubber tree plantation in Vietnam. Death could hide behind each tree.

Fertile soil, warm days, and beautiful country. War ruins it all.

PART II

NOT SUPPOSED TO DIE

BURIED ALIVE

As Waggie headed for Quon Loi, bodies stacked high, blood spilling from the open doors, Waggie forced the shuddering aircraft toward safety. Roy was placed right behind the pilot. Sammons was doing what he could for the wounded. Warrant Officer Darling had taken that hit in the shoulder but was still able to assist with the wounded and was helping Sammons separate the living from the dead.

Roy was lying on his left side, his sawed-up forearm under him, the weight of his body stopping the blood flow - somewhat. His right hand was trying to hold his intestines in place. Evidently, the hole from the hit he took in the back had torn open almost to the front of his chest as he strained to lift the wounded and/or in his hand-to-hand fight with the NVA. His face was covered with blood, the dried blood clotting out all vision. He couldn't speak; the rifle butt that didn't actually break his jaw, snapped something that prevented him from talking.

The blood-loss from his wounds also took its toll on his strength; he had been in that melee for over *six-hours*. He was going to live, he felt, or did he feel anything? His iron will forced him to be positive at all times.

The pain was intense. "*God, how it hurt*," he remembered. "I felt like my entire body had been set on fire. It was a combination of stinging pain, of a feeling that I was being tortured, ripped apart bit by bit as if I was being drawn and quartered between horses. I was sick to my stomach but knew I didn't dare throw up or my intestines would come out. I couldn't talk; I don't think I wanted to. I was afraid all my teeth would fall out."

His right forearm was bleeding profusely. The little nick the NVA took from it required about a dozen large stitches. He recalls only the racket the chopper was making, hoping it would land soon. Within 20 minutes it landed at Quon Loi.

As the extraction slick bounded to a rough landing with its double load of bodies, medics began moving the wounded. Others took care of the dead. Bodies were piled in a stack like cord wood.

"I could hear everything going on," Roy explained. I heard the *'aw's* and *whew's*' and a dozen other comments, all signifying the carnage in that small aircraft."

"I could see too, through a small slit in my left eye that wasn't completely covered by blood. I tried to speak. I don't remember what it was I wanted to say, but I couldn't mutter a sound, my jaw was frozen shut.

"A medic was standing over me, then came down on one knee beside me. *'What about him?'* a voice asked. Through that lone peephole in my eyelid I saw him shake his head no. *'He's pretty bad. Better leave him alone.'*

"Pretty bad? I guess I *was* pretty bad but I had no intention of dying. It had been too long and too hard a trip to get where I was. I refused to die. But it was getting harder and harder to breathe. My mouth wasn't functioning and I sucked in air through my nostrils. I knew I was leaking blood from everywhere. Blood was slipping from my mouth, blood was pouring from my right arm but my left arm was okay, tucked under my body. It was hot and I was sweating and blood mixed with sweat made more blood, just a lighter color and a bit thinner. I couldn't move my legs but I knew they were there; the numbness hadn't taken over completely. As the medic tripped on one of my legs, I felt it. No, I'd be all right. I just hoped they'd get to me soon.

"I could feel the wetness of the blood covering me. It was my own blood plus that of the leaking corpses still in the slick. I think all the wounded were taken out, I was one of the last. But I wasn't there alone with the wounded; the pain was there. It was ever-present, unyielding.

"I felt my intestines oozing under my right hand, seemingly trying to get air - to breathe themselves - and to exit my body in search of room to spread out and rest. I tried to shake that thought from my head.

"'*Look at this,*' I heard someone say. '*Get those stretchers over here, on the double.*' More men got into the chopper. '*These three dead ones ain't ours,*' one voice said. '*They're NVA.*'

"The thought bothered me. In my haste and in the heat of battle, I guess I picked them up too. No matter, the trooper said they were dead. I felt my body being lifted as sunlight again showered my face. They had finally gotten to me.

"'*Put that one over there with the other there. He's had it,*' I heard one of them say. Had it! What does he mean *had* it? I wasn't dead. Were they planning to zip me in one of those airtight, plastic bodybags? Oh no! I had come too far for this. I had no intention of dying. If the NVA couldn't do it, it would not be by my own troops *this* way.

"Being of Yaqui Indian heritage, I guess I did look like an Asian. My eyes weren't exactly round and were slanted a bit. I was five foot six and I weighed about 145 pounds. My skin was brown. I couldn't say anything. I couldn't even move.

"They laid me on the ground next to the dead NVA, the

guys I had loaded by mistake. A bodybag was being fitted under my feet and the sound of the zipper as it crossed over my knees caused me to summon all my remaining strength. With a prayer to the Lord, I managed to gurgle - spit maybe - hoping someone would see it. Someone *did* see it!

"*'Hey! That's Benavidez. That's no damn gook. That's Sergeant Benavidez. That's Roy right there,'* the familiar voice of Master Sergeant Jerry Cottingham barked out just as the medics were about to suffocate me in one of those rubberized bags of death. I could see them load the three NVA's in bags and I was next. I shudder when I remember the sound that bodybag made as it was being shaken open just before they lifted my feet to put me in it.

"The Lord gave me strength one last time and my buddy, Jerry Cottingham, a reconnaissance team leader I knew well, recognized me. I now owe my life to several people; Leroy saved me weeks ago. Waggie surely saved my life by risking his under the threat of certain death; Darling and Smith saved me by volunteering to work the door guns, and now Cottingham. Yeah, strange as it seems, I knew somebody *'up there'* was watching over me. I wonder why? I guess I'm just not supposed to die."

* There were 7,547,000 "assault sorties" flown by the U.S. Helicopter Pilots during the Vietnam War.

* The U.S. lost 2,257 airplanes, and 4,869 helicopters from June of 1967 to June of 1973.

ANOTHER CLOSE CALL

On the chopper flight to Saigon, Roy had been loaded in a stretcher and placed on the floor with the other wounded. The medics were rushed and only had time to wipe Roy's face, clean up some of his wounds, and load him back on the chopper. They knew if he was going to live, he would have to get expert help fast.

Lying in a stretcher next to Roy was Mousseau. Roy reached for him and managed to grasp his hand. Neither man could speak, and it pained Roy to turn but he forced his head to the right to look at his comrade who was looking back with a blank stare from the only eye he had left.

Just before landing in Saigon, Roy felt Mousseau's fingers clawing into his hand. Mousseau's arm was twitching and jumping and as Roy looked at his friend, the grip slackened and Mousseau's hand went limp.

"*No, Mousseau! Don't leave me now,*" the words screamed in Roy's brain. "*We've been through too much. We're almost home man - don't die! Please Frenchy, don't go now.*" As he tried to talk to his dying friend, tears streamed down Roy's cheeks.

Benavidez lifted his head and tried to scream for help but words were impossible. He managed to gurgle again and blood spilled over his chin, the same action that saved his life at Loc Ninh.

The pilot heard the attempt at words and yelled to his co-pilot. "*My God! The guy's strangling. Do something!*"

"The co-pilot was next to me, over me, on his knees and about to stick his knife in my throat to free my windpipe. I made some sounds, while spitting and sputtering blood, and managed to nudge the co-pilot toward Mousseau, directing him with my eyes and slight toss of my head. In a short time, he pulled my hand from Mousseau's and shook his head. He placed Frenchy's arm under the blanket, then pulled the blanket over Mousseau's head. I laid there with tears streaming down my cheeks until I was unconscious."

It took a team of surgeons several days to remove most of the metal from Roy's body. Roy doesn't remember any of it. His first recollection was waking up and "feeling sore all over, being bandaged like a mummy, tubes sticking in every opening in my body, and looking into the familiar face of Brian O'Connor, lying in the bed across from me. He was bandaged as much as I was and neither of us could talk or move, only look and wiggle our toes at each other. Each morning we woke up, we used this toe-wiggling to tell the other that we were still alive."

The days and nights that followed aren't that clear in Roy's memory, but he does recall waking up one day in another ward. O'Connor was gone and Roy had no way of knowing if he was alive or dead. Roy was being operated on much of this time. Twice they reopened Roy's side looking for bullet fragments and found some too near his heart to remove. The doctor's report I examined tells of *two unspecified foreign objects* lodged *in* his heart! They are still there. The surgeons also removed a large piece of shrapnel that took out his right lung.

After three weeks Roy was transferred to a hospital in Japan by way of Ambulance Bus ride to Tonsunhut, Vietnam and on to Tokyo for a longer stay at the service hospital there. After several weeks in Tokyo, Roy was transferred back to the states. Hurt but still stubborn, Roy insisted he be allowed to walk to the helicopter that took him to the airbase and then to the plane that was to fly him home. He *came* to Vietnam on his feet and, by God, he would *leave* on his feet. Then, across the Pacific to the west coast and cross-country to Texas and Beach Pavilion at

Brooke Army Medical Center in San Antonio where he stayed for almost a full year.

Roy called me when he read my finished manuscript and complained about a few inaccuracies, the worst one being on the first page about *twenty-eight* wounds in his body. He quickly pointed out that he had but *five* real wounds made by bullets. In checking with his doctors and looking at his x-rays and medical charts, I discovered there were, in fact, over *forty* holes the size of a green pea or larger, not counting the bayonet slashes.

To set the record straight, there were but five *bullet wounds*. One bullet went clean through his calf, another that was dug from his right thigh, one bullet in his left thigh, the round that entered his lower back and exited under his left armpit, two hunks of bullet from his right buttocks but close enough together where it could have been but one. *"Surgeons were taking metal out for days, and I don't think they kept count. I was opened up a bunch of times,"* Roy added. *"All I could do was lie there and let them take out what they could."*

Roy still has metal *"working its way out now and then,"* like the small sliver he took from his nose during that dinner we attended, or the one working its way out of his scalp just below his hairline, or the other that is pushing its way out of his right forearm.

I didn't count the bayonet slashes either but I imagine they can be put down as *wounds*, like the one to his right arm that left a 6-inch long scar, or the one on his left arm that is a series of scar tissue where the enemy bayonet sawed into it three or four times. The slash on his left wrist can't be counted either; that's where doctors operated and removed some tendons from his wrist and finger so his left forearm would be mobile.

ROY P. BENAVIDEZ' WOUNDS
May 2, 1968

FRONT VIEW

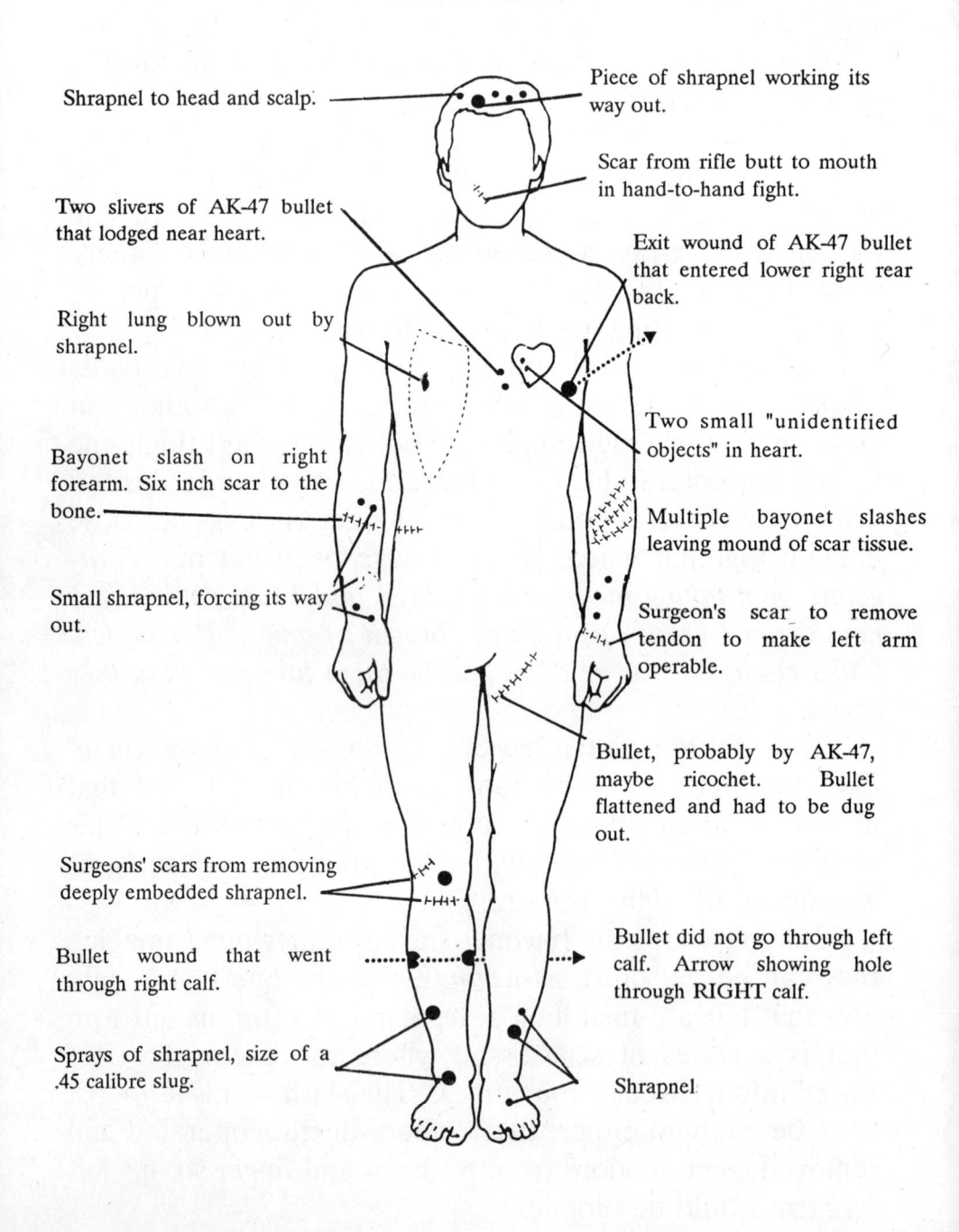

Shrapnel to head and scalp.

Piece of shrapnel working its way out.

Scar from rifle butt to mouth in hand-to-hand fight.

Two slivers of AK-47 bullet that lodged near heart.

Exit wound of AK-47 bullet that entered lower right rear back.

Right lung blown out by shrapnel.

Two small "unidentified objects" in heart.

Bayonet slash on right forearm. Six inch scar to the bone.

Multiple bayonet slashes leaving mound of scar tissue.

Small shrapnel, forcing its way out.

Surgeon's scar to remove tendon to make left arm operable.

Bullet, probably by AK-47, maybe ricochet. Bullet flattened and had to be dug out.

Surgeons' scars from removing deeply embedded shrapnel.

Bullet did not go through left calf. Arrow showing hole through RIGHT calf.

Bullet wound that went through right calf.

Sprays of shrapnel, size of a .45 calibre slug.

Shrapnel

ROY P. BENAVIDEZ' WOUNDS
May 2, 1968

REAR VIEW

Scar from enemy rifle butt.

Path of AK-47 bullet. Roy was bending over picking up Wright. Arrow shows path of bullet horizontal to ground.

Shrapnel lodged in head and neck. Large marks denote metal removed. Smaller signifies still embedded.

Shrapnel scars, some pieces removed, some still embedded.

Maybe piece of shrapnel that blew out right lung.

AK-47 rifle bullet "tumbled" as it entered Roy's lower right back. Large scar from wound tearing during hand-to-hand combat and from four operations.

He did, however, feel two hard slaps on his right buttocks that slammed him to the ground. To be accurate you may subtract one or two marks from this chart. And maybe add a dozen more BB-sized pieces of shrapnel too small to illustrate.

Small shrapnel in right hand.

Additional shrapnel in back of knee. Removed by surgeons leaving "nickle-sized" scar.

These three wounds were either large shrapnel or bullets. Surgeons dug out metal & report wasn't specific in listing.

There is a combination of <u>fifty-seven</u> scars, holes, bayonet slashes and pieces of shrapnel marked on this chart. One or two marks on the right buttocks could have been made by the enemy mine that telescoped Roy's spinal cord the first time he was hit in 1968

Cache of enemy weapons.

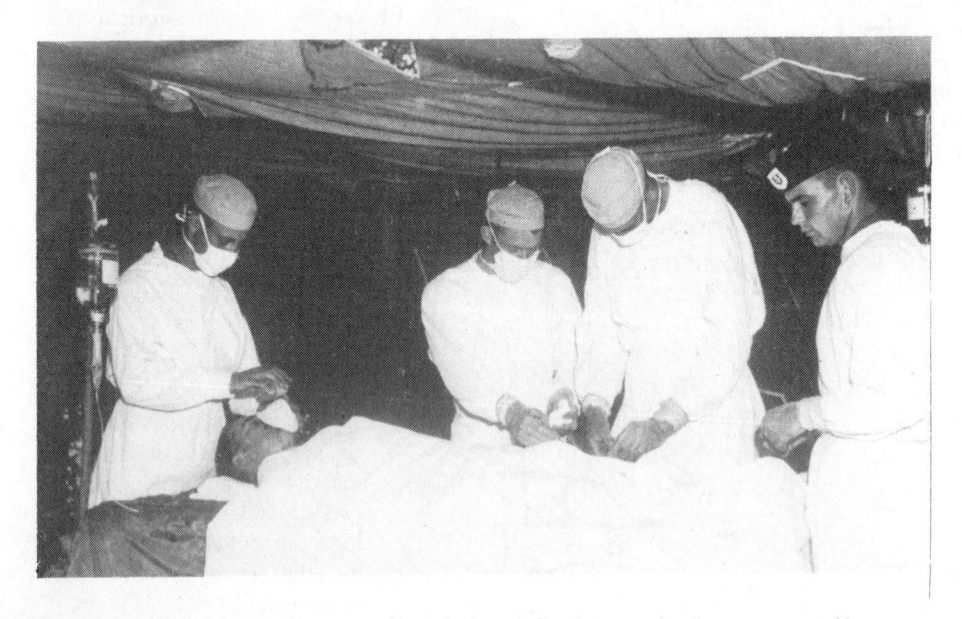

Doctors in emergency field hospitals and chopper pilots saved many lives.

THE DISTINGUISHED SERVICE CROSS

Only weeks prior to being released from the hospital at the Beach Pavilion of Brooke Army Medical Center, Roy was visited by a young lieutenant who came to hand out medals to patients. Of a fistful of Purple Hearts he handed *four* to Roy. From a list, he handed out several Bronze Stars, and a few Silver Stars. After handing out the various medals, almost as an afterthought, the young officer stopped.

"Oh, I almost forgot this. This is yours too, Sergeant," he said to Roy. Roy slowly opened the box and displayed, lying on a velvet background, was the Distinguished Service Cross!

For his six-hours in Hell, for all the pain, the wounds, the agony, fright, frustration...the fact that he *volunteered* to jump in an area that promised certain death, he was being awarded the *second* highest medal his country could offer, a DSC. The award was handed to him like a grocer gives bubble gum to a polite kid, or like a *"Donut Dollie"* from the American Red Cross serves a cup of coffee to a thirsty GI.

Roy accepted the medal and thanked the young officer for bringing it to him. His thoughts were not on the medal but in getting better and continuing his career in the Army.

A male nurse - the ward master - a Staff Sergeant who had attended to Roy, promptly told Roy that such a medal can only be given out by a *flag officer*, a general at least. *"Hey Lieutenant,"* the orderly called. *"This isn't right."* The medic took the medal from Roy and chased after the officer to tell him the rules on presenting such a medal. When the orderly returned - *without the DSC* - Roy wondered if he had actually been awarded the medal at all.

On September 15th, 1969, General Westmoreland, now Chief of Staff of the U.S. Army, presented the Distinguished Service Cross to Roy in a formal ceremony at Fort Sam

Houston. It was still only the second highest medal for bravery above and beyond the call of duty, second only to the Congressional Medal of Honor, but Staff Sergeant Roy P. Benavidez accepted it graciously and wore it proudly.

General Westmoreland presents the Distinguished Service Cross to his former driver on September 10, 1968, just four months after Roy's six-hour battle in hell.

THE HOSPITAL

Being in the hospital was not new to Roy. A few years prior, just before Christmas day in 1965, he was attending a Bob Hope Christmas Show. The next thing he knew, he was in a hospital bed at Clark Air Force Base in the Philippines flat on his back, paralyzed from the waist down.

Trying to piece together exactly what happened was difficult; he could only guess. What he did know was he last recalls trying to get a close seat at the show. One minute he was in Vietnam, and when he awoke, twenty-five days had passed, and he was at the Beach Pavilion of the Brooke Army Medical Center at Fort Sam Houston in San Antonio, Texas...a short auto-trek from his home in El Campo.

Yes, this was a new one on Roy and his doctors. He reasons he must have been on a recon mission disguised as a VC and wearing their black pajamas when, apparently, he stepped on a mine. He was found lying in the jungle by a Marine Recon Patrol, unconscious. Dogtags were found sewn in the lapel of the pajamas.

To this day he cannot remember *how, why, where,* or *when*. His injuries were uncertain. The only marks were a large bruise, a giant X on his right buttock, and another discoloration on his left knee. Whatever hit him telescoped his backbone and snapped his spinal cord. Nothing was severed and nothing crushed. But he was paralyzed and had significant loss of hearing in his right ear and a numbing in his sense of taste, a condition that exists as I write.

"A team of surgeons proclaimed I'd never walk again, but I did. It wasn't easy but I was determined not to spend the rest of my life in a wheelchair. At night, when everyone was asleep, I'd tumble from bed and crawl, using my elbows, hands and chin to pull myself across the tiles of that always-waxed floor and try standing against a wall."

Roy spent five months in that hospital. A few days

before the Fourth of July in 1966, he walked out *on his own two legs*! Four months later, the determined Green Beret made *three* parachute jumps in one day to requalify for jump pay and assure himself that his military life was not going to confine him to a desk or to some officer as a permanent driver.

In May of 1969, after that battle in Cambodia, almost a full year after being wounded severely and repeatedly, Sergeant Roy Benavidez walked out of Brooke Army Medical Center hospital a second time and was assigned temporary duty at Fort Devens, Massachusetts, headquarters of the 10th Special Forces Group. He made one more parachute jump but the pain was too great. The cold weather forced his transfer to Kansas but the winters there were terrible and made his wounds react so intensely he would wake up at night from the pain.

But Roy didn't want to be discharged from the army; it was his life. He even went on two field exercises with the 1st Infantry Division from Fort Riley, in West Germany, but his wounds made him hurt so much that he was simply not capable of taking the punishment. Back at Fort Riley, Roy met General Patrick Cassidy who noticed the DSC ribbon on Roy's uniform and asked if Roy would like to move to a warmer climate and be his driver; back to Fort Sam Houston again but *not* in the hospital. Roy was at Fort Sam until his Honorable Discharge on September 10th, 1972.

* Roy called just a few moments ago and told me that he was going to San Antonio tomorrow (January 12th, 1990) to attend the funeral for General Patrick Cassidy.

RECEIVING THE MEDAL OF HONOR

Thirteen years later, after what could be an entire book on red tape, regulations, and frustration, now-Master Sergeant (Retired) Roy P. Benavidez was honored at a formal ceremony at the Pentagon in Washington, D.C. On February 24th, 1981, he was presented *the* highest award offered to a combat soldier given by his country; the blue ribbon with white stars supporting that beautiful gold medal was draped around his neck by then-President of the United States, Ronald Reagan, in a formal ceremony before several thousand people.

The President read the citation himself, the first time that I can find a president actually "*read*" the citation. But President Reagan was so moved by this heroic soldier that after he hung the Medal of Honor around Roy's neck the President reached out and gave Roy a hug. It startled this combat veteran who returned the hug but not without stepping on Mr. Reagan's *foot* with his mirror-shined combat boot.

The ceremony was glorious. The honor guard, the service personnel, and 39 of Roy's family and friends were flown to attend the ceremony. At long last, 13 years after he earned the medal, Roy P. Benavidez *had* the MEDAL OF HONOR.

This final award came about only when the Army Medal of Honor Board received a letter from Brian O'Connor, the brave radioman Roy thought had died. He was living in the Fiji Islands for those missing 13 years and his personal letter to Ronald Reagan was the final link in the long chain to Roy receiving the Medal of Honor. O'Connor was the lone other survivor anyone could find from that mission. Wright and Mousseau were dead. If any of the CIDG's survived, they would probably be in hiding because of the North now seeing in complete control of their country.

It was a miracle that O'Connor learned of Roy's dilemma in being awarded the MOH. But, Fred Barbee, publisher of the *El Campo Leader-News*, had written a gut-wrenching story about Roy titled, "*Roy Benavidez...Sometimes Patience Wears Thin.*" The story was so inspiring and so well written, that it was picked up by several major newspapers including the *Dallas Morning News* and finally in *The Army Times* and other veterans newspapers. It made its way overseas. One morning a local resident in some part of Australia picked up the paper and read Fred's story about Roy. It was Brian O'Connor - '*Big Team*'.

"I'll never forget that telephone call," Roy told me. "I didn't know if O'Connor had made it. He was so shot up. But when I heard the words, '*Tango Mike Mike*', my heart took a wild leap and I had to choke to stop from crying. That nickname was given to me by O'Connor after I won a quick wrestling match with a Vietnamese years before. I was just about his size and he wanted to wrestle for fun. I had my mind set that I'd let him win after a brief encounter, you know, for good will. But when he knocked my Green Beret off in jest, I didn't like it so I put him down in a eyeblink. From that day on, O'Connor called me *Tango Mike Mike*, code for *That Mean Mexican*."

* "*Greater love has no man than to lay down his life for his friend.*"   John; 5.13

RECEIVING THE MEDAL OF HONOR 93

Big Team and *Tango Mike Mike* meet again.

Fred Barbee and Roy showing story that brought Roy and O'Connor together again after 13 years.

Roy meets the President and First Lady.

Roy and "friend" review honor guard.

RECEIVING THE MEDAL OF HONOR

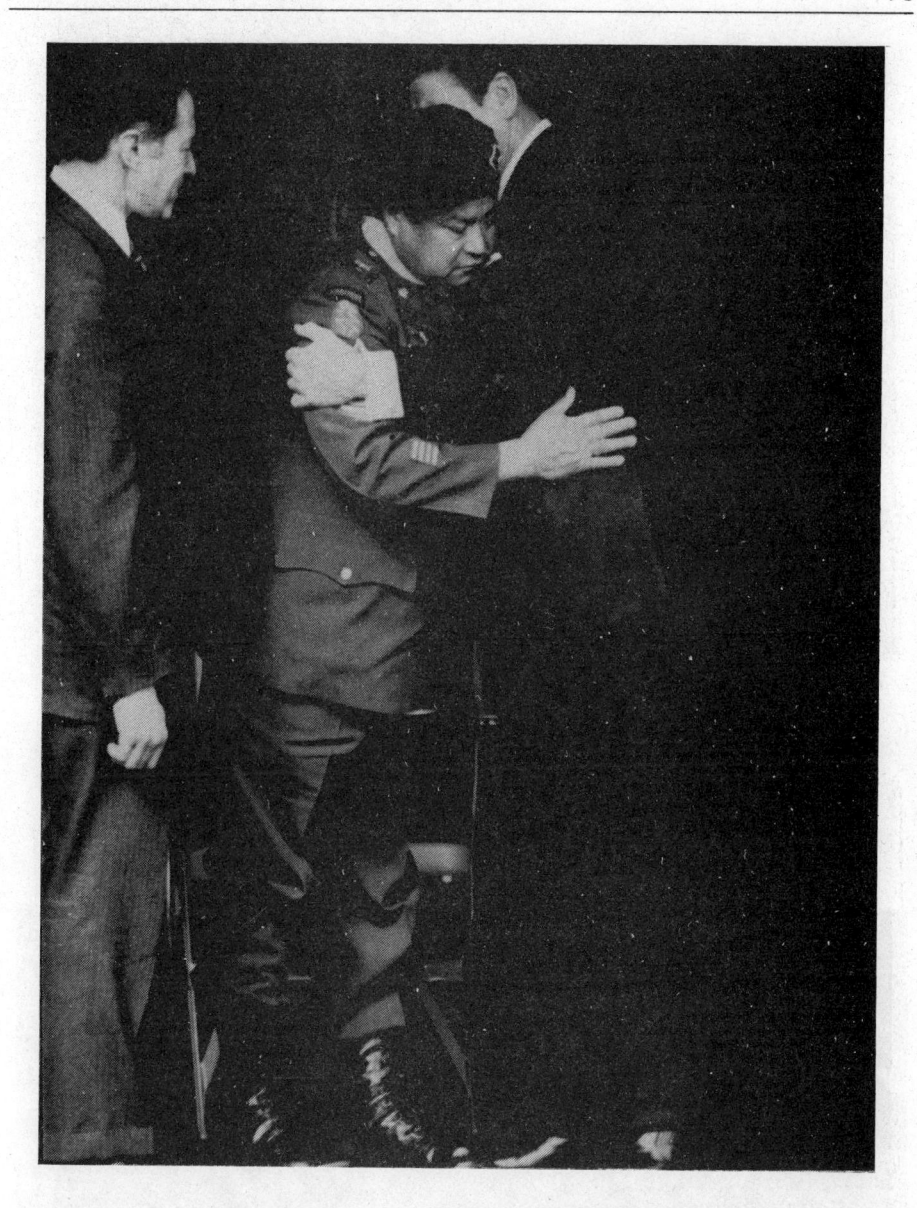

Secretary of Defense, Caspar Weinberger looks on as President Reagan reached out to hug Sergeant Benavidez. Roy was planning to step back to salute but recovered, managing to step on only the BIG toe of his Commander-in-Chief with his highly-polished combat boot.

President Reagan, Roy, and Brian O'Connor.

The Joint Chiefs of Staff stand at attention for the last Medal of Honor recipient.

ALWAYS A SOLDIER

Each day of Roy's life he has a schedule to follow, a regimen just the same as when he was in the military. He still gets up at the crack of dawn when he takes his first walk of the day, maybe three miles. He does it for exercise, and he does it to ease the constant pain he experiences.

He gets telephone calls too, maybe 15 a day. Even though he has an unlisted number, he gives it to anyone who asks for it. And he gets letters from everywhere, maybe as many as 20 a day. He answers each one.

The letters are usually from groups around the world asking him to make a speech here, to appear there, to address a Rotary club, a Veterans organization, or even the opening of a Hispanic shopping center. He gets letters from people who see him on television, hear his voice over the radio, or read about him in the newspapers. He receives letters from veterans, former Special Forces buddies, mothers of veterans, or letters from school kids. He likes the ones from kids the best and keeps them in a filing cabinet.

Roy keeps these letters - or at least he did keep *all* of them until his wife issued him an ultimatum, "Either rent a storage place for all of these papers or stack them in your bedroom and *you* live in the storage shed."

What a woman she is! A book should be written about her. You see, she too, is a hero. She has stuck by this guy through all of it. She knew he was a special person but most of all she knew and accepted the fact that he was already married - *to the Army*! She knew he loved her but she also knew he loved the army. She didn't always agree with what her hero husband wanted but she always went along with it, usually with minimum complaint.

Her name is Lala, or at least that's what Roy calls her.

He real name is *Hilaria*. She knew how much Roy wanted to be a paratrooper and she knew it wouldn't stop there. No, next was becoming a Green Beret and finally, she knew he *volunteered* for Vietnam. She didn't know he also volunteered to get close to where the fighting was, and she had no idea whatsoever that he volunteered to go into that hellfight on May 2nd, 1968.

But then, I guess Roy didn't know about that either because he calls it, "*doing his duty*" or that other explanation he gave me he called *Involuntary Reflex Action*. That's what I do when a fly buzzes around my face; I swipe at it to stop the annoyance. *That* is my definition of Involuntary Reflex Action, not going into an impossible situation where the chance of survival approaches *zero*.

Lala is special as are each of Roy's three kids. Apparently, the example he personally set for his children, the conduct he exemplified to his family, and the care and rearing his lovely Lala did on these fine, wonderful youngsters, made these young people on par with the Cosby kids on television.

Their oldest daughter, *Denise*, just received her degree in Business Management from Wharton County Junior College. *Yvette*, the next in line, is a sophomore at that same school, with a straight "A" average. In high school she was a member of the National Honor Society. *Noel*, their 17-year old son, is graduating from high school in El Campo. Roy is so proud of him and hopes he will enter West Point, but Noel seems set on Texas A & M. Roy and Lala feel Noel is old enough, and bright enough, to choose for himself.

Roy has been approached by no less than two-dozen producers, investors, directors, etc., to make a movie of his life. What they wanted were the war scenes because war sells movies. Roy is considering it, but *only* if he has some control on what goes into this movie. He doesn't want any obscene language (you notice there is none in this book) because, though not a director, he feels a good movie does not have to display vulgar language. Besides, as a role-model for the young, he wants to promote decency.

Yes, Roy Perez Benavidez, son of a sharecropper who completed only the 7th grade, has become *somebody*. He received his GED for high school graduation in the army. After his retirement he received an Associate Arts degree from Wharton Junior College in Texas. He has become an accomplished, much sought-after public speaker and he *is* a national hero. Humbly, he feels he is fortunate to be able to travel and influence youngsters. As long as his health allows, he will continue his quest for many years to come.

I did promise Roy, if he shared some of his life with me, I'd print this piece about our flag. If you've read it before, read it again. If you haven't, please pay close attention to each word. My friend, the recipient of THE LAST MEDAL OF HONOR, Roy P. Benavidez, asks that of each of you.

Benavidez at Fourth of July parade in San Antonio with former Texas Governor Mark White and former Mayor of San Antonio, Henry Cisneros.

Roy at West Point, giving hints to cadets on Special Forces tactics.

HELLO, REMEMBER ME?

Some people call me Old Glory; others call me the Star Spangled Banner. But whatever they call me, I am your Flag, the Flag of the United States of America. Something's been bothering me. I thought I might talk it over with you, because it's about you and me.

I remember, not too long ago, when people lined up on both sides of the street to watch the parade and naturally, I was leading every parade, proudly waving in the breeze.

When your daddy first saw me coming, he immediately removed his hat with his right hand and placed it against his left shoulder so his hand would rest directly over his heart. Remember that?

And you, you were younger then, I remember you standing there straight as a soldier. You didn't have a hat but you were giving a hand right salute. Remember your little sister? Not to be outdone she was saluting the same way as your dad, with her right hand over her heart...remember?

What's happened? I'm still the same old flag. Oh, I have a few more stars since you were a boy, and a lot more blood has been shed since those parades of long ago but now, I don't feel as proud as I used to. When I come down your street in the same type of parade, some of you stand there with your hands in your pockets and I may get a small glance from you, but you oftentimes look away. And I see your small children running around and shouting and playing. They don't seem to know who I am or what I represent. I saw one man take his hat off and look around and when he didn't see anybody else with their hats off, he quickly put it back on.

Is it a sin to be patriotic anymore? Have you forgotten what I stand for and where I've been? Anzio, Guadalcanal, Bataan, Korea, and Vietnam. Take a look at the Memorial Honor Roll sometime. You'll see the names of those who fought to keep this country free, those who bled and suffered and died for those of you who are standing, not saluting, not telling your children about me.

Remember these words?...One Nation Under God... When you salute me you are saluting these brave people who have, in fact, given their tomorrow's so you could have your today's.

Well, it won't be long before I'll be coming down your street again. So when you see me, think about what I just told you. Think about what I stand for. Stand erect, place your right hand over your heart, and tell your children and friends to do the same. As you salute me, I'll salute you back, by waving to you. And I'll know that...YOU REMEMBERED!

Unknown author

* Sister Maria Veronica sent this poem to Roy. She has been the keeper of the records at the Medal of Honor Grove in the Freedom Foundation at Valley Forge, Pennsylvania.

Now, in 1990 he is Brigadier General (left.) Robin M. Tornow

B-56 teammate of Roy, "Ski" Ledzinsky, *"Dai-uy"*, (Vietnamese for captain)

B-56 Special Forces Camp

PART III

HEROES

ROGER DONLON

Many heroes were never awarded a Medal of Honor, or any other medal for that matter. Some of these were overlooked because a commanding officer failed to submit the information, some because there simply were no live eyewitnesses, and many more because so many have performed acts of bravery *"above and beyond the call of duty"* on a daily basis.

But some deeds are so heroic, so uncommon, so profoundly valorous, that these people are awarded the medal that is the highest symbol of bravery at certain personal risk to their own lives. Their performance was accomplished so heroically against all odds that everybody should know of their deeds. Such was the case with Roger Donlon, Captain, U.S. Army, Special Forces, 7th Group, Detachment A-726 on July 6th, 1964.

Captain Roger C. Donlon was always meant to be military. As a young boy he was a troop leader in the Boy Scouts. In high school, he dreamed of the military. Even his home in Saugerties, New York was just up the Hudson River from the U.S. Army Military Academy at West Point.

Roger Donlon entered New York State College of Forestry at Syracuse University. After a year he joined the U.S. Air Force, in December of 1953. After two years in the Air Force he was accepted into West Point in June of 1955 where he left after 2 years. In February of 1958 he was selected to attend Infantry Officers Candidate School at Fort Benning, Georgia and received his commission as second lieutenant in June of 1959.

Lieutenant Donlon was selected for Special Warfare School at Fort Bragg, North Carolina and became a Green Beret, a member of Special Forces. In May of 1964, now a Captain, Roger Donlon was in command of an 11-man team of Green Berets and sixty Nungs (ethnic Chinese mercenaries who fought for the Americans) at Camp Nam Dong, a Special Forces Detachment, A-726, 30 miles northwest of Da Nang, close to the borders of Laos and North Vietnam. A detachment of just over 300 ARVN soldiers (Army of the Republic of Viet Nam) was also in camp along with many civilians - wives and children of many of the Vietnamese soldiers.

This was one trying time for a combat soldier. The Americans were sent as *"advisors"* and were not allowed to fight in combat, to lead the ARVN, or even issue orders; all they could do was *"suggest"* things.

On the morning of May 6th, 1964, Captain Donlon alerted his troops for trouble. A recon patrol a few days prior gave reports that civilians - villagers - were in fear and refused to talk. He knew trouble was coming.

At exactly 2:26 in the morning, as Captain Donlon stepped through the screen door of the mess hall, a large explosion from a mortar round knocked him back through the door. The attack had begun.

The camp was surrounded by a double barbed-wire fence and the "*outer*" camp was the responsibility of the ARVN, the South Vietnamese soldiers. Most of the surrounding countryside was heavy woods and sparsely populated, a perfect spot for concealment and surprise attack. Mortar rounds could be zeroed in with little trouble by the VC.

The "*inner*" camp was manned by the Green Berets and Nungs. A flare fired by Sergeant Michael Disser showed hundreds of men rushing the camp from all sides, somewhere between 800 and 900 strong.

His citation reads like this: "For conspicuous gallantry and intrepidity at the risk of his life above and beyond the call of duty while defending a military installation against a fierce attack by hostile forces, Captain Donlon defended against a reinforced Viet Cong battalion as they launched a full-scale, predawn attack on the camp. During the violent battle that ensued, lasting 5-hours and resulting in heavy casualties on both sides, Captain Donlon directed the defense operations in the midst of an enemy barrage of mortar shells, falling grenades, and extremely heavy gunfire. Upon the initial onslaught, he swiftly marshalled his forces and ordered the removal of the needed ammunition from a blazing building. He then dashed through a hail of small arms fire and exploding hand grenades to abort a breach in the main gate. En route to his position he detected an enemy demolition team of 3 in the proximity of the main gate and quickly annihilated them. Although exposed to the intense grenade attack, he succeeded in reaching a 60mm mortar position despite sustaining a severe stomach wound. He had been blown from the mess hall by that first mortar, blown off his feet by a second mortar as he raced for the 60mm mortar position, and a third mortar blast picked him up and slammed him to the ground, where he received shrapnel in his stomach and left forearm.

"When he discovered most of the men in the gunpit were wounded, he disregarded his own injuries, directed their withdrawal 30 meters away, and stayed to ward off any further attackers. Noticing that his team sergeant was unable to evacuate the gunpit, Donlon crawled toward him. While dragging his fallen comrade to safety, another mortar round exploded wounding him in his left shoulder. Although suffering from multiple wounds, Captain Donlon carried the abandoned 60mm mortar weapon to a new location 30 meters away where he found three wounded defenders. After administering first aid and encouragement to these men, he left the weapon with them, headed toward another position, and retrieved a 57mm recoilless rifle.

"Then, with great courage and coolness under fire, he returned to the abandoned gunpit, evacuated ammunition for the two weapons and, while crawling and dragging the urgently needed ammo, received yet another wound to his leg from an enemy hand grenade. Despite his critical physical condition, he then crawled 175 meters to an 81mm mortar position and directed firing operations which protected the seriously threatened east sector of the camp. He then moved to an eastern 60mm mortar position and, upon determining that the vicious enemy assault had weakened, crawled back to the gunpit with the 60mm mortar, set it up for defensive operations, and turned it over to two defenders with minor wounds. Without hesitation, he left this sheltered position and moved from position to position around the beleaguered perimeter while hurling hand grenades at the enemy and inspiring his men to superhuman effort. He refused aid to his wounds. There was no time.

"As Captain Donolon bravely continued to move around the perimeter, a mortar shell exploded, wounding him in the face and body. In the eerie light of a VC flare that brought a momentary lull to the fighting, a loudspeaker told the Americans to put down their weapons. *The VC going to take camp and all be killed.* The many comrades around Donlon said their captain resolved to go down fighting and quickly directed a volley of rounds toward the area of the loudspeaker. Sergeant Disser took Donolon's direction and landed a round right *on* the speaker.

"The long awaited daylight brought defeat to the enemy forces and they retreated back to the jungle leaving 54 of their dead, many weapons, and grenades. Captain Donlon immediately reorganized his defenses and administered first aid to the wounded. *One hundred fifty-four* VC were killed during the fight and over *fifty* ARVN and Nung died. *Two* Americans died and *seven* were wounded.

"His dynamic leadership, fortitude, and valiant efforts not only inspired the American personnel but the friendly Vietnamese defenders as well, and resulted in the successful defense of the camp. Captain Donlon's extraordinary heroism at the risk of his own life above and beyond the call of duty are in the highest traditions of the U.S. Army and reflect great credit upon himself and the Armed Forces of his country."

Donlon spent a month in a hospital in Saigon where his visitors included General Westmoreland and Ambassador Maxwell Taylor. In his first battle Donlon had led a magnificent fight, and word of his exploits quickly spread.

When he recovered from his wounds, Donlon rejoined the surviving members of his team. They completed their six-month tour in Vietnam in November of 1964 and flew home together.

The nine survivors gathered with Donlon at the White House on December 5th, 1964, Where President Lyndon Johnson presented Captain Donlon with the MEDAL OF HONOR.

Donlon was justifiably proud of his team members. "*The medal belongs to them, too*," he told the president. As of December 1987, Roger C. Donlon is a full colonel, close to retirement. He went back to serve another tour in Vietnam and is one of the *seventeen* Special Forces men to receive the Medal of Honor.

Yes, ROGER C. DONLON was the *first* recipient of the Medal of Honor in Vietnam. ROY P. BENAVIDEZ is the *last*.

B-56 Special Forces Camp somewhere in Vietnam.

HISTORY OF THE MEDAL OF HONOR

The MEDAL OF HONOR is the greatest tribute for bravery America offers to a member of its Armed Service who has distinguished himself above and beyond the call of duty. It is a military award for those who perform an act of heroism while risking certain death. This book tells of some of those recipients of this prestigious medal.

As early as 1847 Congress awarded a *Certificate of Merit* which added an additional two dollars per month to any soldier who distinguished himself in battle. Five hundred and thirty-nine men received Certificates of Merit during the Mexican War. However, no award could actually be *worn* to signify their heroic act and people had to learn of this honor by word of mouth.

Recorded history states War Secretary Gideon Welles was trying to find a method to stimulate his sailors by awarding a special tribute to their courage and bravery in battle. On December 21st, 1861, President Abraham Lincoln signed Public Resolution 82, and the Medal of Honor became law. In 1863, Congress made the Medal of Honor a permanent decoration.

Prior to the Medal of Honor, the first recipient of "*a*" medal was General George Washington, presented to him by the Continental Congress for his part in driving British forces from Boston in March of 1776.

The first medals awarded to soldiers for individual action were given on November 3rd, 1780, to three militiamen by the Continental Congress for their capture of a British spy, Major John Andre, who was on his way to meet traitor Benedict Arnold. These three silver medals were not for gallantry in combat but for saving the country from "impending danger."

Those awarded the Medal of Honor are in a rather select group of heroes. Of the millions of serviceman, only

222 of the 3,394 recipients are alive today. In the United States Army, for instance, only 5 Medal of Honor recipients are still on active duty.

Being awarded the medal is certainly not without complications. A board decides who will receive the Medal of Honor. This board consists of five retired general officers for the purpose of investigating who is (and is not) worthy of this medal. From October 16th, 1916, through January 17th, 1917, the board *rejected* 910 names of those already awarded the medal. Of these 910 names, 864 were from the 27th Maine Volunteer Infantry in one regiment during the Civil War.

The criteria for the Medal of Honor, once awarded for *"gallantry in action and other soldierlike qualities,"* was changed to read *"for conspicuous gallantry and intrepidity in action at the risk of life above and beyond the call of duty."* *"His"* also stands for *"hers"* since a woman was once awarded the medal.

Criteria demand that two eyewitnesses observe the action. The valor and risk of life must be *so* outstanding that there is no doubt that the danger to personal life was in dire jeopardy. The gallantry performed must be *"above and beyond the call of duty"* to clearly distinguish this brave act from a *"lesser form of bravery."*

Further, a recommendation for an Army or Air Force medal must be made within two years from the date of the deed that warrants the medal and the award must be made within three years of the deed. The Navy Medal of Honor must be made within three years and the awarding of the medal, within five years.

The term *"Congressional Medal of Honor"* has been changed to simply *"Medal of Honor."* It is a medal presented by a high official "in the name of the Congress of the

United States" and thus the word *"congressional"* preceded the medal. It was customary for at least a member of congress to pin the medal on a recipient, but the highest honor is when the President of the United States presents it.

MEDALS OF HONOR

ARMY   AIR FORCE   NAVY & MARINES

TEN HISPANIC MEDAL OF HONOR HEROES

(left to right).."most" of Cleto Rodriguez; Colonel Jay Vargas; Lucian Adams; Joe Rodriguez; Jose' Lopez; Louis Rocco; Roy Benavidez; Alejandro Ruiz; Silvestre Herrera and Rudolfo Hernandez. These men represent three wars... plus the fact that Hispanics are courageous and proud.

* In Vietnam, 238 were awarded the prestigious medal: 12 from the Air Force; 14 from the Navy; 57 Marines, and 155 from the Army.

A WOMAN RECEIVES THE MEDAL

"The Medal of Honor has had strange bedfellows," a general once wrote, "and Mary Walker was one of the strangest. But never doubt it for a moment that she was as deserving of it as anyone."

Mary Walker became a physician in 1855, one of the first woman doctors in the country as well as one of the youngest; she was barely 22. She believed strongly in women's rights and spoke out about them often.

When the War Between the States began in 1861, Dr. Mary Walker applied for an army commission but, being a woman, was turned down. *"Only men fight wars,"* newspapers quoted men in a poll as saying in those days. Mary took the next best route and volunteered at a hospital in Washington for several months. In November of 1862 Mary was accepted by Major General Ambrose Burnside as a volunteer field surgeon to help tend the sick and wounded. Mary was elated at the opportunity although not being awarded a rank.

Dr. Walker operated on and treated the wounded for almost two years. She walked around Union front lines clad in gold-striped trousers worn by army officers and a green sash and a straw hat with an ostrich feather sticking from it. She took care of the wounded at Fredricksburg in 1862, and a year later, she was tending casualties at the battle of Chickamauga.

During this time, Dr. Mary Walker applied for a commission. She felt she was a part of the military and wanted recognition as such. She was working side-by-side with men - surgeons like her - but they had a commission and she did not. But times just weren't ready for a "lady in the army," and a medical board in Chattanooga, comprised soley of men, pronounced her "utterly unfit for the position of medical officer."

Her break into the army wasn't until Major General George H. Thomas appointed her to replace the assistant surgeon of the 52nd Ohio Infantry when the unit's that doctor was killed.

Dr. Mary Walker tended soldiers and civilians for most of the war. She was even suspected as being a spy for the Union at one time. One army communique refers to her *"secret services"* for the North and another states *"she gleaned information behind enemy lines that saved Major General William T. Sherman's forces from a 'serious reverse' during a battle."*

Mary was captured by the Rebels and sent to a prison in Richmond only one month after joining the 52nd Ohio. She spent four months in prison before being *"traded"* for a Confederate officer. She took great pride in this *"man-for-man"* exchange as it was noted on the record books. She could not become a legitimate officer because she wasn't a man yet, she was traded *equally* for a man once imprisoned.

After her release from jail, Dr. Mary was granted a contract as an acting assistant surgeon at $100 a month and awarded back pay for her service with the 52nd Ohio but she was not given her desired commission as an officer. The army denied her request for battlefield duty, and she spent the remainder of the war practicing at a Louisville female prison and a Tennessee orphan asylum. Because of her abrasive manner and abrupt demeanor, she offended many. She believed in equality and fought for it almost every day of her life. She was rude and outspoken, and women were not supposed to act like that in those days. She refused to comply with *"what was"* and tried to make things the way she felt they should be.

Although paid in full and released from government contract, Mary lobbied for a brevet promotion (a commission advancing an officer in honorary rank without pay or command) to major for her services. Her request was denied. "How could she expect the rank of major when she hadn't any rank at all," one statement read, said to have been penned by Secretary of War Stanton. "It was impossible to give a rank - to a woman yet - who was never, officially, ever in the armed services."

Walker persisted in her request. After several angry letters to President Andrew Johnson, the President and Stanton decided to *"throw her a bone"* and ordered a Medal of Honor to be given to her as a reward. *"Anything to quieten her."* Mary Walker wore that medal over her heart for the rest of her life.

After the war, Mary devoted her time to many unpopular causes including women's rights. She wore men's pants and opposed smoking. She was taken to court many times for violating *"proper decorum"* expected of a woman. She was dismissed of all charges and oftentimes left the courtroom amidst hearty applause.

Her private practice was never successful. By the mid-1880's, she was living on a government pension and had been reduced to side-show existence. She did various novelty acts and spoke on women's rights and the advantage of women wearing long pants, all the time wearing the Medal of Honor on her lapel. Many observers became indignant. They reasoned she had been awarded the medal for pity and not for actual combat experience. She became a thorn in the sides of *"real men."*

In March of 1893 one Ohio newspaper stated, *"There was a time when this remarkable woman stood upon the same platform with Presidents and the world's greatest women. There is something grotesque about her appearing on a stage built for freaks."*

In 1901, Dr. Mary Walker, now nearing 60 years of age, nearly lost her pension by circulating a petition asking clemency for the anarchist who had assassinated President McKinley. But her greatest disappointment was yet to come.

In 1916 Congress revised the Medal of Honor standards to include only "*actual combat with an enemy*," and several months later a board of army officers rescinded 910 medals awarded during the Civil War. Mary's medal was included. The board took back her medal, citing her ambiguous military status and the fact that her "*service does not appear to have been distinguished in action or otherwise.*" She was then advised that it was a crime to wear her medal. She vowed to continue wearing it every day she so pleased.

For the following two years Mary applied to congressmen and War Department Officials, but with no luck. On one of these visits, ironically, she suffered a bad fall on the Capitol steps. She never fully recovered and died on February 21st, 1919, at the age of 86.

The army review board of 1916-1917 set a precedent of criteria for the Medal of Honor. A recipient of this medal now had to meet this stringent criteria. No more would medals of this magnitude be "*handed out.*" But, the case of Mary Walker was not forgotten. Nearly sixty years after her death, at the urging of a descendant, the army restored her medal. This review board apparently felt Mary was deserving. Thus, Dr. Mary Walker goes down in history as the first and only woman to ever be awarded THE MEDAL OF HONOR.

SERGEANT YORK

Young Alvin York was tall and slim with red hair. He was born in a one-room log cabin in Pall Mall, Tennessee, a small village in the Cumberland Mountains, on December 13th, 1887. He was the third of 11 children.

His father, William York, was a blacksmith. Alvin helped his father and worked on the family's farm. Everyone in those days hunted and had to be good with firearms. William was such a good shot that when the county held sharpshooting contests, they asked William to *judge*. If he entered, he would surely win. And Alvin was said to be even a *better* shot than his dad.

"My dad threatened to muss me up right smart iffin' I hit a turkey in the body 'stead of the head," Alvin told an army buddy, "or iffin' I didn't take a squirrel's head off with one shot. We needed the meat for our bellies."

Young Alvin was barely literate. He attended school only three weeks each summer for five years, which amounted to about a third grade education. He was not the religious and pious person Coop showed him to be in the movie. He was just the opposite. Or rather, he *was* just the opposite for much of his young life.

By his own admission, he was "*always spoilin' fer a fight*." And he was a drinker and a brawler and always carried a revolver and a knife. He gambled and often came home "drunk as a saloon fly."

Meeting Grace Williams changed his life. Grace was the daughter of a neighbor whose family was religious and whose parents frowned on her even *thinking* of dating that wild, good-for-nothin' Alvin York. So Alvin found religion.

One story quoted Alvin York's feelings on the life he had been leading. "I began to pray to God to help me as a poor sinner to find some relief from my appetite fer drink, cigarettes and tobacco, card playin', swearin', dancin' and fer all the things the world had that a man couldn't do as a Christian and my sins were pardoned on January 1st, 1915." Alvin was 27 years old at the time.

In August of 1914 when World War I began, Alvin was safely tucked away in his little mountain village and didn't quite understand "fightin' people way over there. They wasn't botherin' nobody round here." When America declared war in April of 1911, Alvin was a patriot but had to decide between his country and his religious beliefs. He wanted no part of war, he just wanted to be left alone and with the help of his church pastor. He declared himself a *conscientious objector.*

On November 15th, 1915, Alvin was inducted into the Army and reasoned he'd "jes go to that ol' camp and say nothin'. I did everythin' I was sposed to do but I was sick at heart jes the same."

Alvin was assigned to Company G, 328th Infantry, 82nd Division, a newly-created group comprised of officers and men from every state in the Union. York wrote home. "They even put me by some Greeks and I-talians to sleep. Most of 'em never tetched a gun before and missed everythin' cept'n the sky."

His religious beliefs caused him to not want to kill anyone because of the Bible. But his commanding officer, Major George Buxton, had some long talks with Private York and finally convinced Alvin, by using some bible verses (Luke 22:36..."*He that hath no sword, let him sell his cloak and buy one.*") that war was sometimes necessary and York became a combat soldier.

On October 8th, 1918, near Chatel-Chehery, France, Alvin York was a corporal in Company G, 328th Infantry, 82nd Division. It was the first month of the Meuse-Argonne offensive. This day, the sharpshooter from Pall Mall,

SERGEANT YORK

Tennessee became the "*Greatest hero of that war.*"

The colonel who was in command that day told the entire story: "We were pinned down by German machine gun fire from the top of a ridge. York pressed forward on his own, shooting enemy soldiers whenever they appeared from trenches. He was a sharpshooter; if he could see them he could hit them. I don't recall any turkey-gobbling by Corporal York; that, I feel, was the work of the newspaper reporters. There was too much noise going on all the time to hear such a noise.

"The corporal worked his way up and around, shooting when he saw someone and we could only watch. The machine guns were firing continuously. A german major, apparently feeling he was surrounded, promised to order his troops to surrender if the killing would stop. He couldn't believe it when he saw that *one man* was doing all the shooting. In less than three hours, York had silenced *thirty-five* enemy machine guns, killed *twenty-five* German soldiers and captured *one hundred and thirty-two* prisoners. When we saw them walking out, hands behind their heads, weapons thrown down, we couldn't believe it. I still don't believe it to this day but, it happened. We all saw it!"

During the battle, York was rushed by a German lieutenant and five of his men in a sort of *suicide charge*. York had been "tetching off every German who raised his head and this young german lieutenant knew York's clip held but five shots. As the group came closer, York chose a method he used at home with turkeys; he shot the *last* one *first* so the others who were in front didn't know what was happening. After he had leveled the back five with his 5-shot clip Enfield, he took out his .45 and shot the front man.

When the troopship pulled into Hoboken Dock on May

22nd, 1919, York was swarmed by photographers, dignitaries, and spectators. He was rushed to the Waldorf-Astoria Hotel and given a suite adjacent to the one reserved for the president. An onslaught of attention and adoration was heaped upon this new hero from the mountains, and York wasn't accustomed to this type of treatment. Who was? He had been promoted to the rank of sergeant and became known worldwide as Sergeant York, "*the*" hero of World War I. And what was York's first request? He wanted to call home and talk to his ma and to his galfriend, Gracie. Next he wanted to ride on a subway. "He had heered of 'em but had never seen one."

On his return to Pall Mall, Alvin York was presented with a 400-acre farm by the State of Tennessee. He and Gracie were married on their new farm with over 3,000 onlookers in attendance.

York converted to the Church of Christ in Christian Union and turned down a honeymoon in Salt Lake City calling the journey "merely a vainglorious call of the world and of the devil." The couple honeymooned at home on their new farm.

Through the years, York stayed in his hometown, worked his farm, did some blacksmith work, and taught Bible school. Politicians visited him regularly at election time, and he posed with them in pictures. He was even asked to run for the vice presidential nomination of the Prohibition party in 1936.

In typical York logic he explained to those who asked how he was able to get so many Germans to surrender. "*I jes surrounded 'em*," he answered. When a general once remarked that he must have captured the entire German army, York bowed his head, tipped his hat, and answered as humbly as he had about almost everything else. "*No, I only got 132 of 'em."*

At age 54, when World War II broke out, Alvin York volunteered for active duty. "If they want me, I'm ready to go," the military hero was quoted as saying. "I'm in a mighty different mood now from before that other war," he said. He was never called to war but did serve as head of the local draft board and sent two of his sons off to war.

At the age of 77, America's most famous hero died, in Nashville, at a veterans hospital. Alvin York - *Sergeant York* - one of the most famous recipients of THE MEDAL OF HONOR.

General Douglas MacArthur. "Old soldiers never die. They just fade away."

MacARTHUR GETS THE MEDAL

This Medal of Honor is one of the few in history to be awarded for "*no particular battle*" but cited that General Douglas MacArthur as being "personally courageous in the face of bombing attacks in Corregidor, for conspicuous leadership in preparing the Philippine Islands to resist conquest, for gallantry and intrepidity above and beyond the call of duty in action against invading Japanese forces, and for the heroic conduct of defensive and offensive operations on the Bataan Peninsula. He mobilized, trained, and led an army which received world acclaim for its gallant defense against a tremendous superiority of enemy forces in men and arms. His utter disregard to personal danger under heavy fire and aerial bombardment and his calm judgement in each crisis inspired his troops, galvanized the spirit of resistance of the Filipino people, and confirmed the faith of the American people in their Armed Forces."

The general received his Medal of Honor on April 1, 1942, in Australia. In acknowledging the medal, MacArthur said, "*he felt this medal was intended not so much for me personally as it is a recognition of the indomitable courage of the gallant army which it has been my honor to command.*"

MacArthur's father received the Medal of Honor seventy-six years prior for "*rallying Northern troops on November 25, 1863, at Missionary Ridge, Tennessee, during the Civil War.*" The MacArthur's are the only father and son to both receive THE MEDAL OF HONOR.

* "*I would rather have the Medal of Honor, than be president of the United States.*"

President Harry S Truman

AUDIE MURPHY

Twenty-four military decorations. He received his Medal of Honor on June 2nd, 1945.

AUDIE MURPHY

What a sweet, babyfaced kid he seemed to be. Movies always depicted Murphy as being kind, considerate, and non-violent but plenty able when the situation called for action. This was THE Audie Murphy in real life. This was *the* Audie Leon Murphy who was the *most* decorated hero in World War II.

Audie Murphy was born in Hunt County, near Kingston, Texas. As a soldier, he didn't look like much, certainly not a hero but then, what exactly *do* heroes look like? What distinguishing marks appear on a person that tells you he is a hero? The answer, *none*! Heroes come in all shapes, sizes, and colors. They are neither short nor tall, smart nor illiterate. They are people who respond to a certain situation when others do not.

In interviewing dozens of Medal of Honor recipients, in being an invited guest at a recent Medal of Honor function in Chicago, I looked around and found not one clue as to *why* any of the men risked his life against certain death to save his comrades or obey his orders. It is a reaction, they told me. It was nothing they actually *thought* about doing.

"*Audie Murphy was not soldier material*," his drill sergeant said. "He was short, skinny, didn't need to shave with only 'peach fuzz' on his face, and certainly not '*hero-looking*' material. His commanding officer in boot camp wanted him to be a cook. Another officer wanted him to get a job in the PX but he convinced him that he wanted to be a combat infantryman. Reluctantly, they conceded."

As a private he served in North Africa and proved to be an adept and resourceful soldier. He obeyed orders and was capable of giving orders. He was fearless, and an expert marksman. He volunteered for everything regardless of the danger.

His movie, *To Hell and Back*, was near-accurate also, void of obscenities and full of cute little quips. But the recounting of his battle was not in the hands of the directors. He wanted to make the movie as near accurate as he could...and he did.

Murphy advanced though the ranks. His company, B, 15th Infantry, 3rd Division was casualty-depleted and Murphy rose to the rank of second lieutenant. He spent twenty-four months of fighting from farmhouse to farmhouse, in woods and in open fields and proved his effectiveness in combat.

On January 26, 1945, Murphy led his men to the forefront of an American attack on a German position in the village of Holtzwihr, France. His orders were to wait for support on the snow covered frozen ground about a mile outside the village. He had two armored tank destroyers, each with a turret cannon and a .50 calibre machine gun.

At two that afternoon, six German tanks rumbled out of Holtzwihr, fanned out in an open field that lay in front of Murphy's position and ground their way toward the allies position. Enemy infantrymen, wearing white camouflage cover, followed the tanks. As the Germans advanced, one of the American tank destroyers slid into a ditch while maneuvering for fighting position, its cannon now pointed uselessly at the ground.

The German tanks opened fire on Murphy and his men. A round burst in the trees above his machine gun squad, killing the men and disabling the gun. Another round blasted into the second tank destroyer and set it afire. Survivors from the crew poured out the hatch and ran for cover.

By radio Murphy called for artillery fire. When the rounds fell behind the advancing tanks, he called in for coordinates closer to his own position. American artillery rounds began to find the ranks of German infantry, but the tanks passed on, untouched, spraying the Americans with machine gun fire. Murphy ordered his men to fall back.

He now faced the advancing Germans alone. He fired his carbine at the infantrymen until he ran out of ammunition, then jumped on the burning tank destroyer and blasted away with its machine gun. When the Germans were virtually on top of him, Murphy called artillery in fire *on his own position*. Reports came in that Murphy continued to call in coordinates and say "*correct fire*" watching where the rounds landed and calling in new coordinates. The barrage turned back the attack.

Miraculously, Murphy survived the attack. He crawled down from the tank destroyer unscathed. He suffered only a small wound from shrapnel in his left leg, a wound from the day *before*. He felt it was too insignificant to require medical attention.

The tank-destroyer exploded minutes after Murphy limped away toward the rear. There he rejoined his men and organized them for a successful counterattack against the Germans.

Murphy fought for three more months, until the Germans surrendered. One June 2nd, 1945, he received his Medal of Honor, the most prized of his World War II decorations. He killed or wounded about 50 of the enemy that one day. In all, his honors list 24 military decorations including the Medal of Honor. He personally killed 240 Germans in combat in Sicily, Italy, and France.

In 1945 Murphy appeared on the cover of *Life* magazine. Actor, James Cagney called him and urged him to come to Hollywood, and in 1948 Audie Murphy starred in a film titled, *Beyond Glory*. He acted in a total of 39 movies.

Although he netted about $2.5 million on movies, Audie Murphy went bankrupt from poor investments. If you recall, he always walked with a slight limp, the result of a hip wound he received in combat after gangrene had set in.

After the war, Audie Murphy suffered 50% disability from shrapnel in his legs, a nervous stomach, insomnia for several years and constant headaches. Yes, the war had taken its toll on this young hero, before *and* after. It oftentimes does.

In May of 1971 at the age of 47, Audie Murphy died in a plane crash that took the lives of four others and the pilot. His suffering was now ended.

* *"Bravery is not the absence of fear, but the ability to keep going in the presence of fear."*
Jesse Mendez

CAPTAIN SAMUEL FUQUA

The first recorded Medal of Honor for World War II was the Navy MOH awarded to Captain Samuel Fuqua for his bravery "*above and beyond the call of duty with risk to his own life*" when he served aboard the *U.S.S. Arizona* as it burned and sank during the Japanese sneak attack on Pearl Harbor, December 7th, 1941.

His first recollection of danger was sirens. When he came topside, he was thrown back and knocked unconscious by a bomb blast that left a gaping hole in the deck of the *Arizona*. Upon regaining consciousness, Captain Fuqua began a three-hour bout of calm bravery amidst all the chaos. He recalls seeing bombs dropping from high-level bombers "*like large balls of hail falling from the sky*." Bombs were striking the deck and exploding below in the engine room. Crew members were coming from below and began jumping off the ship. Some were wounded, some on fire, and many blinded. Fuqua and other uninjured crew members knocked them unconscious thus preventing them from certain death by drowning.

Fuqua supervised and commanded; he was calm in the face of danger and death. When the bomb that struck the *Arizona* next to the bridge penetrated the forward magazine room, the ship "*erupted like a volcano with debris and bodies flying in all directions.*" More than 1000 were estimated to have been killed in that single explosion. Fuqua stayed and fought the fires, took command, and put wounded aboard undamaged lifeboats. That one blast was so powerful that it hurled over 100 men over from the *Vestal*, an ammunition tender that was moored alongside the *Arizona*.

Captain Van Valkenburgh and Admiral Kidd had been killed aboard that firey inferno on the *Arizona*, which began to sink. Only then did Captain Fuqua give the order to abandon ship. Fewer than 200 men from the 1400 on board survived that day. In all, fifteen men received the Medal of Honor for that first day of heroism and devotion to duty. Captain Samuel Glenn Fuqua from Laddonia, Missouri, was awarded his medal for, "*his amazing cool and sound judgement in the face of such danger, inspiring all who saw him which undoubtedly resulted in saving the lives of many.*" Captain Van Valkenburgh and Admiral Kidd were awarded Medals of Honor posthumously.

Medal of Honor recipients at annual Salute to America's Heroes weekend, sponsored by the Illinois Vietnam Veterans Leadership Program in Chicago.

CUSTER

Custer received *two* Medals of Honor. Not "*the*" General George A. Custer but his brother, Second Lieutenant *Tom* Custer, and for deeds on two separate days that involved the capture of an enemy flag. It was during the Civil War, and capturing the enemy flag was a deed of honor and courage.

On his first flag-capture, Lieutenant Tom Custer of the 6th Michigan Cavalry took the flag in a fight at Namozine Church on April 2nd, 1865. He repeated the feat four days later as General Henry Capehart witnessed Tom and his troops charging the enemy. Young Tom spied the waving Confederate banner and rode directly at it. The Confederate who had the flag fired point-blank at Custer, hitting him in the face. Custer fired with his pistol killing the soldier and made off with the flag. Later at the Union encampment his brother, the General, was appalled at the sight of his wounded brother, bullet wound in the cheek and neck, riding in with the flag. Tom wanted first aid and to go back into the battle. His bravery inspired others in battle. For capturing *two* flags, Tom received *two* Medals of Honor. Eleven years later Tom was killed beside his brother, General George Custer, at Little Big Horn.

* *"I'd give my immortal soul for that medal."*
General George S. Patton

MOH recipients Benavidez and Sasser see each other often. Roy's home in El Campo is but 60 miles from Rosharon, where Clarence Sasser lives. They both volunteer for celebrations, dedications, and personal appearances at schools or veterans organizations. Their "war" ended more than two decades ago but they still talk about freedom and patriotism; two prime examples of what you can accomplish, regardless of race, creed, color or ethnic background. Both are heroes and true Americans.

CLARENCE SASSER

Clarence Sasser is a Medal Of Honor recipient from Texas. He lives in Rosharon, just 15 or so miles from Houston. He was Private First Class in the Army with Headquarters Company, 3rd Battalion, 60th Infantry, 9th Infantry Division. On January 10th, 1968, PFC Sasser was serving as a medic aidman with Company A, 3rd Battalion, on a reconnaissance operation in Ding Tuong Province, South Vietnam. When the battle began, within minutes the American casualties numbered over thirty. Sasser ran across an open rice paddy under small arms, recoilless rifle, machine gun, and rocket fire from well-fortified enemy positions to aid the wounded. He helped one man to safety and took shrapnel from an exploding rocket that tore through his left shoulder. He refused medical attention and ran back across this field with the enemy still firing where he tended wounded and stayed to look for more wounded. Sasser received two other wounds, immobilizing his legs. He dragged himself toward another soldier more than 100 meters away and he treated him, then encouraged another group of comrades to drag themselves over 200 meters to a spot of relative safety. He was weak from loss of blood and in pain from his multiple wounds, yet he stayed with the wounded and treated them for over *five* hours until they were evacuated.

Clarence Sasser is an African-American, one of several to receive the *Medal of Honor*. He is now working in the Veterans Administration Office in Houston, Texas.

IRON MIKE, the bronze statue of a World War II paratrooper at the entrance of Fort Bragg, North Carolina. "The pride and joy of the Airborne."

DAVID CANTU BARKLEY

The *first* and the *last* United States Army Medal of Honor recipients from Texas were *both* Hispanic. The story goes like this, paraphrased from the Sunday Magazine of the *San Antonio Express-News*, May 21, 1989, written by Craig Phelon.

David Barkley kept his secret 71-years after his heroic deed that earned him the Medal of Honor. David was born, David *Cantu* Barkley; his mother was Antonia Cantu, full-blooded Hispanic, making David Barkley a Hispanic-American.

During World War I, blacks and Mexicans were thought to all be uneducated, either wouldn't follow or couldn't understand orders, and were sent to the rear area for mess duty or dig latrines. But David Barkley wanted to prove his worth and volunteered to swim in the icy waters of the Meuse River on November 9th, 1918. Three pairs of men volunteered to make the swim. The current was too fierce for the first team and they turned back. The second team met heavy enemy fire and they turned back. But now David, part of a two-man reconnaissance team, made the swim. He and his comrade, Sgt. Harold Johnson, made it to the other side and drew maps of the enemy's position, but on the way back across the icy river, Barkley developed cramps and drowned. His partner brought the needed information which aided the allies to launch a successful attack.

Two days later, Germany signed an armistice and the war was over. General John J. "*Black Jack*" Pershing, not forgetting this heroic act, recommended David and his fellow trooper for the Medal of Honor.

Seventy-one years later, Ruben Barkley Hernandez, David Barkley's grandnephew, read a story in the *Express-News* about a ceremony honoring a Navy hospital corpsman killed during the Korean War and it caused him to think about his uncle. Hernandez contacted the Medal of Honor Society and furnished them with papers and family mementos to see if the society would like them for their archives.

Now, David Cantu Barkley is recorded as the *first* Hispanic-American to receive the Medal of Honor. Roy Benavidez is the *last*! Yes, Hispanics have a proud heritage and they continue to serve their country with honor.

* Roy is extremely proud of his heritage. He speaks to many functions sponsored by Hispanics around the world. This statement doesn't mean other minorities are not patriotic, but Roy often quotes: *"You will never see an Hispanic-American burn our flag. If you ever do, I hope he's WRAPPED in it!"*

Fourteen-year old Roy. Is there any doubt that after he squeezes the trigger on this 12-gauge shotgun, that his butt will be resting on the ground?

SERGEANT JOHN PITTMAN

The Korean War, a so-called, "*police action*" or "*conflict*," brought us 131 Medal of Honor Recipients: 4 from the Air Force, 7 from the Navy, 78 Army, and 42 from the Marines. I'll tell you about one seemingly insignificant sergeant from Carrolton, Mississippi, John A. Pittman.

John was in the 23rd Infantry Regiment, 2nd Infantry Division. On June 4th, 1951, Sergeant Pittman distinguished himself in action against the enemy. Sergeant Pittman volunteered to lead his squad in a counterattack to regain "*commanding terrain*" lost in an earlier engagement.

Yeah, "*commanding terrain*." You fight and take a hill or position, usually a mud hump nobody gives a squat about, but to make it sound like something, some genius chose to call it "commanding terrain."

Regardless, all the grunts understand this terminology and know what I'm saying. Many veterans reading this lost friends and comrades and were possibly injured themselves while taking a mud hump only to give it back a day or so later. Sometimes you wonder what is inside the minds of those who make these decisions but, as a soldier, you don't question what you do, you just do it!

Moving aggressively forward in the face of intense artillery, mortar, and small-arms fire, Pittman was wounded by mortar fragments. Disregarding his wounds, he continued to lead and direct his men in a bold advance against the hostile standpoint. During this daring action, an enemy grenade was thrown in the midst of his squad, endangering the lives of his comrades. Without hesitation, Pittman threw himself *on* the grenade and absorbed its burst with his body. When a medical aid man reached him, his first request was to be informed as to how many of his men were hurt.

His intrepid and selfless act saved several of his men from death or serious injury and was an inspiration to the entire command. For this, he earned the *Medal of Honor.*

John Pittman now lives in a small town in Mississippi and wants only to put this time of war behind. He, like many of the other severely wounded, hurts every minute of every day. Another of the heroes nobody seems to remember.

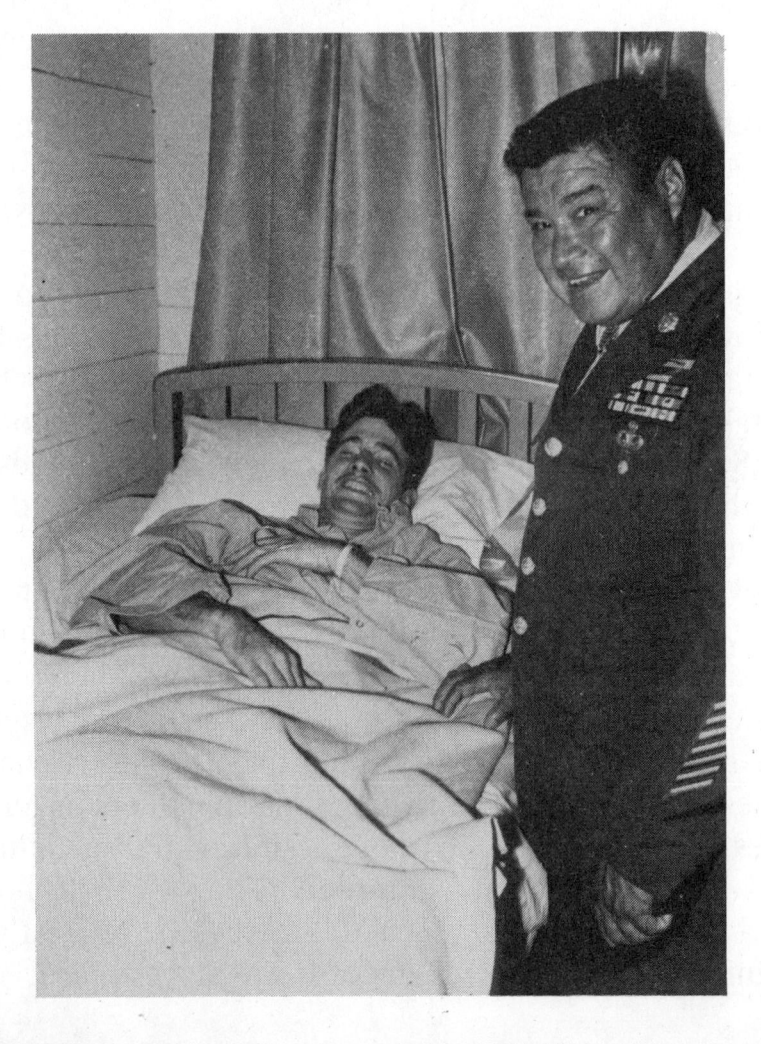

Roy enjoys visiting veterans in hospitals - and they enjoy him.

PART IV

AFTER THE WAR

ROY'S WAR ENDS

Roy's actual war ended on May 2nd, 1968 in Cambodia. But, like those who retire *from* anything, I'd prefer they say they retire *to* something. Such is the case with my friend, Roy Benavidez, Master Sergeant (Retired).

Carrying the *weight* of the Medal of Honor is a responsibility as well as an honor. It's almost like being branded. You are marked as a hero, as a person to be looked up to, respected, and admired. But along with these pluses comes the chore of always being under a microscope - you are supposed to be flawless. During one of our interviews, I taped Roy's thoughts on this matter.

"*I'm just a normal human being,*" Roy told me, "not the least unlike other people out there. I believe devoutly in the Lord, Jesus Christ, and I attend church regularly. I'm a Roman Catholic.

"Most of my life has been spent in the military. I was in a special branch of the military as a Green Beret, a member of Special Forces...and I served in combat. I have done my best to follow the teachings of God, but, being a human I did not follow these teachings to the letter. Oftentimes, God and the military clash on morals. Perhaps I can say I was part of the military some of the time, and a large part of my life I followed the rules of God.

"I do my best not to offend everyone because I love almost everyone. I try in these days, weeks, months, and years since Vietnam, to understand the North Vietnamese, the Viet Cong and even the NVA; including the one who tried to take my life.

"When I think back on that day in May, you know, the day I got hurt so much, I wonder if that North Vietnamese had a family like mine and if he felt he was doing the right thing. It bothers me often when I think of those things because I don't understand it all. Does *anyone* understand it all?

"With these new war movies, the film directors and producers make it look like we were right and they were wrong, the North Vietnamese, I mean. Then other movies show us in a bad light, like raping and pillaging and committing atrocities. I was never in a group like that nor did I even *know* of things like that happening. I don't understand anyone doing such things to other human beings and I can't forgive them for it. There must be some rules, even in war, and I know there were violations on each side. Who began this violation doesn't really matter. Neither I, nor any of the Special Forces I knew was guilty of any of these things. I was just a U.S. soldier doing my duty."

WHY I FOUGHT IN VIETNAM

"In many of the magazines of the armed forces, I oftentimes see a story on Jane Fonda, depicted as *Hanoi Jane*. She was young and foolish in what she did and I try to understand her, but it's a hard thing to do. Many Americans, however, felt and acted in the same fashion as Ms. Fonda. Perhaps you're living across the street - or next door to someone who objected to the war in Vietnam the same as she. Maybe it's wise not to ask around or get into a discussion about this war because you might lose a friend you've had for over 15 years.

"I fought in Vietnam because I was a soldier and I wanted to preserve freedom for my country; a basic reason I know. I also know that many people objected to the war for numerous reasons and I want them to know that I didn't *like* the war. It really does come down to the fact that 'somebody had to do it.' We couldn't *all* refuse to go, to use political influence in dodging the draft, to pursue our college degree, or to run off to Canada. The sickening part to so many veterans is that these people stayed home and enjoyed the freedom while so many of their best friends fought and died. Hating the cause for war, or those who were responsible for the war is one thing, but to stay home wrapped in a safety blanket being woven by the lives of their friends and brothers and *then*, call that American brother a "*baby killer*" or a "*murderer*" is something else. I never understood that.

"One example I remember well was when a general visited us one day (I don't recall his name) but he was telling us of a North Vietnamese who wanted to be the head of a small village in South Vietnam and cared little about what the people wanted, you know, about the same as Noriega in Panama where being the strongest meant right.

"This man from the North warned the villager from the South not to run in the election *or there would be consequences*. The South Vietnamese did not drop out of the election even though his nine-year old son was kidnapped a few days before the final vote tally, the Northern opponent using the child as a hostage.

"On the day of the election as the votes were being counted, the little boy was turned loose and came running and crying from the nearby woods. *Both of his arms had been cut off just above the elbow!* He was screaming for his father as he was running away from the terror and horror and pain inflicted on him by this evil man. When he reached his father's side, he collapsed at his feet and fell to the ground. He bled to death while resting in his father's arms.

"This story was told by a Lieutenant General in the United States Army. I guess *"the other side"* had similar stories but all I know is that the Special Forces veterans I knew were not dopers, rapers, or performed such atrocities that I saw performed on our guys. We would never skin an NVA or VC, nor would we string them up in a tree with their guts ripped out. And I *saw* that! I saw a small child, maybe five years old, who was nailed to the side of a hut because Americans had been kind to her. Her parents were sitting on the ground letting the blood from their daughter's body spill through their hands, trying to experience the last bit of life in the dying body.

"A close buddy in SF had snapshots he took personally of several nuns who had their heads cut off and stuck on stakes outside another village where the nuns only tried to give aid to wounded. I won't describe what they had done before decapitating these Ladies of God, nor will I tell you about the condition of the missionary's body. Whether we were right being in this war is not the question; *they were wrong!* And those of you who feel otherwise are wrong also.

"It was horrible! This war was so different than any other war in history. I know many of you have heard this before, about a 10-year old girl coming up to a GI in the streets of Saigon, smiling and holding a bouquet of flowers behind her back, the same little girl this young GI stopped just yesterday to give her candy. He even took her on a one-block piggyback ride through the streets and she giggled, much the same as his own daughter had done back home.

"All of a sudden, the face on this child changes and becomes contorted - twisted with hate and she says, "*die GI*," as she throws a Russian-made grenade at your feet. But, the grenade is a dud and doesn't explode!

"A week later, in another section of the city, that same little girl is walking up to one of your best friends with flowers held behind her back, a big smile on her face, and a grenade hidden in the flowers. There's too much noise going on and there simply isn't time to yell to warn your comrade. What do you *do*? Do you watch and hope this grenade is a dud also? Or do you level your M-16 and do what nobody sane or civilized would *ever* do? Suppose *you* were this soldier and this seemingly-harmless little girl was walking up to *you*, would *you* want your buddy to shoot? Please do not think this is a fairy tale; it happened many times.

"Perhaps I was naive when I volunteered to go to Vietnam, but I went there to help. We worked with the South Vietnamese people to build schools and roads and taught them modern irrigation procedures. We built churches and hospitals and, oftentimes, those we helped were punished by the North Vietnamese Communists. I wasn't smart enough then to know that there was some other way. I felt that my country needed my help and I volunteered. It was that simple. I didn't have time to think what was right and what was wrong, or why we were there, or what the French did in that country before us. I was an *American*! Communism was a threat to our American way of life and the communist in the North part of that country were forcing their beliefs on those in the South part of that country. Someone had to intervene. And my government, that of the United States of America, a government of democracy and freedom, through the United States Congress and my commander-in-chief, felt our presence was necessary. That is why I fought in Vietnam."

* Roy's unit, the 5th Special Forces Group, was awarded the Civic Action Medal from the Chief of Staff of the Armed Forces of the Republic of Vietnam for their efforts in:

> *Setting up almost 50,000 Economic Aid Projects; 35,000 educational projects; over 35,000 welfare projects; 11,000 medical projects; 1,500 transportation facilities; supporting nearly a half-million refugees; digging 6,500 wells and repairing almost 2,000 kilometers of roads. Also, 130 churches, 275 markets, 110 hospitals, 400 dispensaries, over 1,000 classrooms and 670 bridges. This drawing will show you locations of the various Special Forces camps in South Vietnam.*

South Vietnam

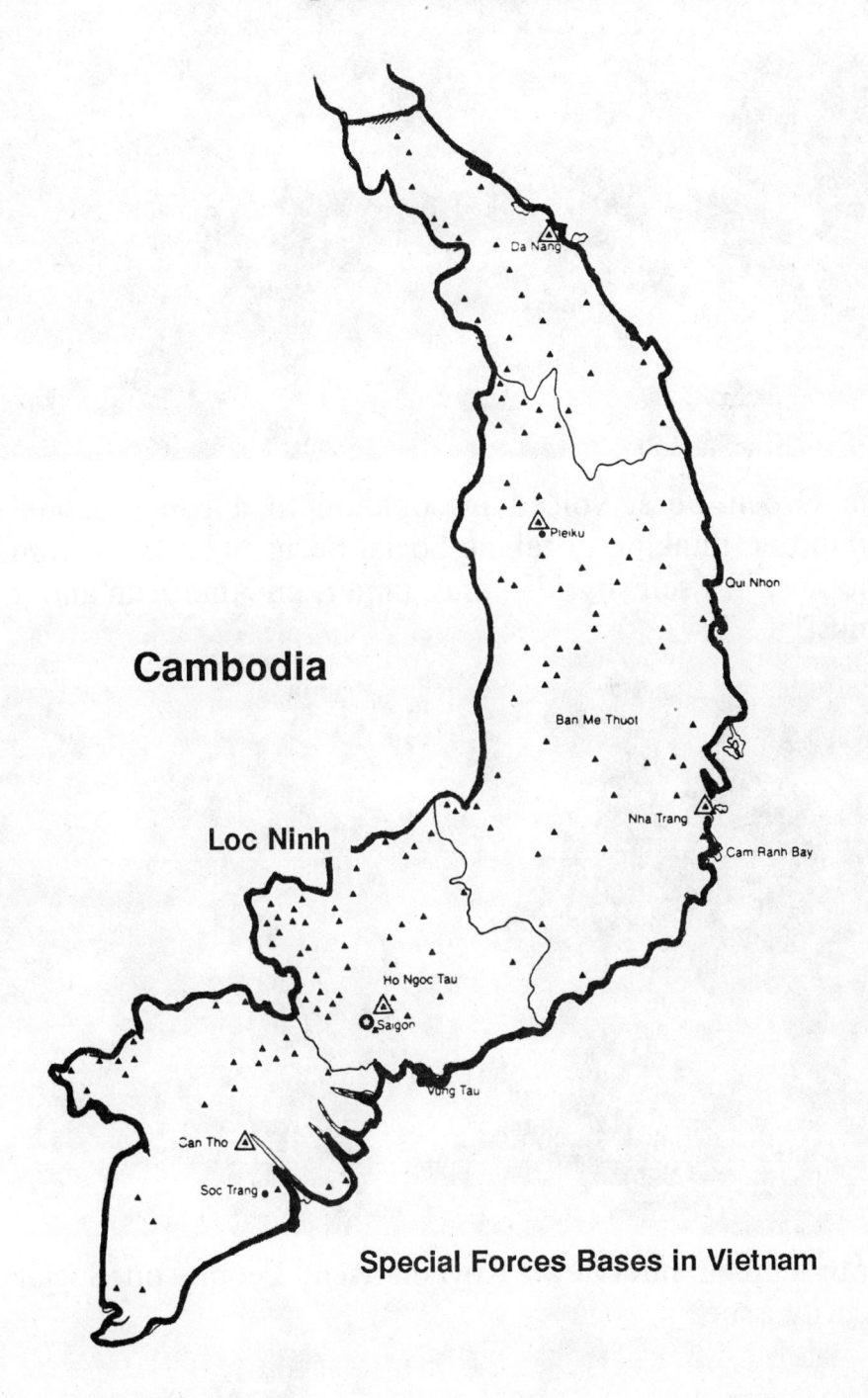

Cambodia

Loc Ninh

Da Nang
Pleiku
Qui Nhon
Ban Me Thuot
Nha Trang
Cam Ranh Bay
Ho Ngoc Tau
Saigon
Vung Tau
Can Tho
Soc Trang

Special Forces Bases in Vietnam

The Green Beret voiced his opinion to a congressional committee thinking of taking Social Security benefits from veterans; "It's selfish, ridiculous, unfair, un-American and it stinks!"

Sarah Purcell interviews Roy on Real People on Social Security issue.

ANOTHER WAR

Perhaps Roy's war in Vietnam had ended, but there were still fights to continue as a civilian. One such *war* came on February 22nd, 1983 when Social Security benefits were about to be cut back. Someone(s), some where, felt that Roy Benavidez and hundreds of thousands like him, should no longer receive government assistance.

"The government apparently felt my wounds had healed and no longer hurt," Roy said. "The fact is, they hurt more today, and will probably hurt more tomorrow, than they did that first day I received them. And the government wanted me to be *tested* to see if I really hurt or was faking it. I went to a doctor in El Campo who said I was unable to work because of my injuries. I was then instructed to go to *their* doctor in Houston. There was also a psychiatrist present. After having me stand and sit, attempt to lift various weights, and poke and prod and take tests, the doctor advised that I was to receive 100% disability.

"One *criteria* was if I could lift a 50-pound weight. My left arm had four operations with tendons taken from my wrist and thumb to make it mobile. There was no way for me to lift much weight with that arm. I had to blow into a tube also but my right lung that had been taken out by shrapnel caused me to flunk that test. Why was I having to endure this humiliation? I think what saddened me most was that tens of thousands of my comrades-in-arms were probably undergoing similar degradation and humiliation. Also, I had been on disability for 7 years and if I had been found not eligible for any number of reasons, I was to have to pay *back* this money I had taken without deserving it. This simply could not *be*. This was the United States of America. And thank goodness it was because I had the right to appeal.

"I wrote a letter to then-Senator John Tower of Texas. Within weeks I was ordered to appear before a psychiatrist and a judge. I took *two and half hours* to tell them of that day in Cambodia. I had to show them the holes and scars and stitches, the mounds of scar tissue, and tell about my comrades who died. Even *that* wasn't enough. The judge sent me a letter to appear before a psychiatrist in Victoria, Texas before he could make a final ruling.

"About this time *Reader's Digest* wrote a story about me. *Real People* picked up the story and wanted me to be aired on television on Memorial Day, May 31st. Then, a reporter from the *Dallas Morning News* asked my opinion on this discontinuing of Social Security. *WOW!* Did *that* please me. I unloaded on him, it hit the papers, and in the following weeks I was flooded with reporters, tv newspeople, and a few letters from Washington, 'requesting my presence.' At all hours of the day and night I was visited at my home by mothers of small children, veterans - desperate people - all asking me to be their spokesperson. 'I was a highly decorated war hero, recipient of the Congressional Medal of Honor, surely the government would listen to me!'

"I was in mental turmoil. I had been a member of the military for twenty-five years. I loved and respected my commander-in-chief, and now I was going to have to say something against my own country? I remembered back, just a few years ago it seemed, that I was just a Mexican-American son of a share cropper. I was refused entry in many restaurants, and had to sit upstairs in the local movie theater. There was no way I could let these 'regular' people down. I felt they needed me, and if I could only tell the politicians my story and how so many needed Social Security, and if my being awarded the Medal of Honor would cause them to listen, then I would talk."

Roy went to Washington, D.C. and he met with many men in three-piece suits. Even news releases spoke of how President Reagan would "*see to it that the private sector aided Roy Benavidez.*" Roy admired and loved his friend, President Reagan, and he knew the intentions of his president were pure, but the idea both pleased and disheartened him. He didn't want *charity*! He didn't want help from the *private sector*. All he wanted for himself, and for the hundreds of thousands of others who depended on Social Security, was to get what they deserved; nothing more, nothing less.

Yes, Washington was aghast. Their many-times wounded, *minority* hero, their Medal of Honor Green Beret, their symbol of what America is about, was now saying *no* to Michael Baroody, deputy assistant to the president himself, about receiving help from the private sector. *Real People* had it all on film! Roy told me what he told that panel that day in one of the meeting rooms in the White House. "*I'm sorry but I can't accept help from the private sector. I just want what me and my buddies are entitled to. These same people who are denying us benefits are living free at the expense of my buddies, their blood, limbs and lives. We just want what we earned.*"

On June 20th, Roy was back in Washington to testify before California Congressman Ed Roybal's committee to broach this Social Security problem. "I was seated behind a small table with my attorney, Tom Burch, a former Green Beret. Tom produced a huge stack of letters I had received in the past weeks from people everywhere asking my help. The group of men judging what I said were in front, sitting behind a long counter-type desk akin to the type in the Oliver North fiasco. I was asked to repeat my story of the letter about having my benefits canceled, my trips to my doctor, the doctor in Houston, the judge and psychiatrist. I told them of the embarrassment and ridicule I felt. I finished by telling them exactly the way my head and my heart directed me." Roy said, "*If my comrades and I are denied these benefits what we deserve, then I ask one last favor. If all of you would please kneel and join me in a prayer to God to save this republic from bureaucratic bungling; if you take these benefits away, there is no hope.*"

Congressman Tom Lantos from California, apparently pleased with such truth, honesty, sincerity, and candor, asked Roy, "In all your testimony, sergeant, you have focused on the military, do you feel it is fair for this government to put civilians - men and women - through the same process that you have been put through?"

"*Sir,*" Roy answered without hesitation, "*if those civilian men and women pay into the Social Security fund, they should also be entitled to those benefits.*" The congressman smiled and asked if Roy was speaking for all Americans who have been so unjustly treated. "*Yes sir,*" Roy replied, "*I come before you, the committee here, and the chairman, to speak for all the American people who are locked in the same situation.*"

New Mexico Congressman Bill Richardson asked Roy if he had it all to do over again, the military career, Vietnam, fighting for his benefits...would he do it. Again, without a moment of hesitation, Roy answered, "*Yes...yes sir. I wouldn't have it any other way. I'd do it all over.*"

HERO STREET

Near East Moline, Illinois lies the small town of Silvis. There is a one-block street in Silvis, formerly called Second Street, that was renamed *Hero Street* just a few years ago, in honor of the heroes who lived on that street.

Between 1910 and 1917 there was constant revolution in Mexico. Many of the inhabitants of that country migrated to the United States and worked on railroads in Texas. As the railroad expanded, the workers followed the work and several families wound up in Silvis, Illinois.

The hardships many of these families endured is written in history books, and this small band of Mexican workers now in Silvis were among those. For several years they lived in the boxcars until they could save enough money to buy property and build houses. The one-block dirt street they settled on was Second Street.

There were 22 families who built their homes on Second Street who were now citizens of the United States. These Mexican-Americans were loyal to their new country and proved it by sending *eighty-seven* of their sons and daughters to war; eight died defending their country.

It wasn't easy on this group of *New Americans* for years, despite their children defending their country. In fact, it wasn't until 1971, that Second Street was paved. But these Mexican-Americans persevered and are now prominent citizens in the area as well as around the country, serving as doctors, lawyers, judges, and leaders in industry.

And Second Street is now *Hero Street*, USA. After a long and hard struggle, this small block of patriots has been honored. At the end of Hero Street is a memorial park, honoring these heroes.

Yes, Hispanics are a proud race of people. Did you know that *thirty-seven* Hispanics have received the Medal of Honor since the Civil War? The *first* man listed in combat who was captured by the enemy in Viet Nam was a pilot named Ed Alvarez, Jr., a Hispanic-American. And the last to *leave* Viet Nam was a Marine security guard named Juan Valdez?

Throughout the history of war, Hispanics have been said to be, "*First to go. Last to leave.*" Many books say, *"When war comes, Hispanics go!"* While visiting the Hero Street Memorial Park, I met a old man who said he was the grandfather of one of the heroes who didn't make it back. He was proud of his grandson, and relayed those feelings to me with this one quote; *"There is something in the bloodline we Hispanics share. We can all look into the face of death and not be afraid, if we are fighting for what we believe."*

Roy signing autographs for high school students in Diboll, Texas.

MARTHA RAYE

"Whew, Pete," Roy told me. "Don't get me started. I don't know when to shut up." And he didn't shut up. I have it on tape.

Of course, I prodded him a bit. It's my job. I asked about Martha Raye. Roy's eyes widened and he continued.

Here is the flipside of the coin to Jane Fonda; Martha Raye. "That is one heckuva lady. I met her; we even had dinner together and I have a picture of us together. The troops called her *Maggie* and I don't know why President Reagan didn't give her the *Medal of Freedom* for all she did for the troops in World War II, Korea, and Vietnam. Maybe if President Bush is made aware of all she did for our fighting men, he'll give her this much deserved and long overdue medal. Put something about her in your book, will you?"

Starting with World War II, when Martha Raye was in her mid-twenties, she began entertaining troops in North Africa, Europe, the South Pacific, on Navy warships, and at Pearl Harbor.

During the Korean War she entertained also, but spent much of her time as an Army Reserve Nurse. In Vietnam, she was *in-country* for two years and spent a total of three years in Vietnam.

At the 1st Medical Battalion, Da Nang, her helicopter was waved off for incoming wounded. She jumped out to help treat a badly wounded marine. She oftentimes performed at small camps and outposts very few ever heard of and shunned publicity for what she was doing. She visited hospitals and aid stations and spent time with wounded soldiers. Her stops in Vietnam included such high-profile places as *Soc Trang, Saigon, Cam Rahn Bay, Danang, Hue Phu Bai, Chu Lai, Nha Trang, Quang Ngai, Pleiku, An Khe,* and the *USS Constellation*.

During Vietnam, Miss Raye was 49 to 58 years old. She was hospitalized one time for anemia, a few more times for physical exhaustion, and heat stroke, but she kept going - entertaining, nursing, and visiting wounded. Because of her visiting these outposts, not only the larger installations, she was lovingly given the nicknames, "*Old Lady of the Boondocks*" and "*Maggie*" and "*Colonel Maggie.*"

From 1965 until 1974, *Colonel Maggie* was in Vietnam. She worked so closely with the Special Forces, she earned the honorary rank of Lieutenant Colonel and was given a Green Beret, a tiger suit, and the Special Forces Insignia. She even made a parachute jump with the 5th Special Forces Group and was twice wounded. She was awarded two Purple Hearts for wounds she received while in combat areas.

At one time she was caught in a firefight near Tay Ninh and a mortar attack at a CIDG-Special Forces camp at Soc Trang in the Mekong Delta. Did she request evacuation? *No*, she stayed to help nurse the wounded. When she returned to the United States, she took letters to wives and families of GI's and wrote to many of them who were still in Vietnam. She hand-delivered over 300 such letters.

There are hundreds of pages written on the good that Martha Raye did for the American fighting man. Let me now list some facts that I feel warrant her receiving The Presidential Medal of Freedom. *Every* combat veteran knows the worth of this great lady who gave so much and received so little. She is 74 years old as I write this book. The troops she entertained and aided through *three wars* would like her to be recognized.

Too often such unsung heroes go unheralded for lack of surviving witnesses or they die before having received their much-deserved honors. Rarely is an oversight corrected before death, but that opportunity exists today. So, President Bush, your friend Roy Benavidez asks this of you.

You remember Roy, Don't you? The first time you two met was in Washington when Roy received his Medal of Honor. Another time, you walked over to him at a gathering in Houston and issued a statement I put on the cover of the book. Roy asks you to look into this Martha Raye matter. He asks it, I ask it, and every past and present member of the United States Army, Navy, Marines, Coast Guard, and Air Force who knows of Martha Raye asks it. And certainly the women who volunteered - nurses, USO, American Red Cross - ask it. *America* asks it!

"Colonel Maggie"

Roy first met George Bush at the MOH ceremony in Washington, DC when Mr. Bush was vice-president. "I love that man," Roy states. "I always knew he was special and now the American people know it. He is a wonderful person, a devoted husband and father, a proud American, and will go down in history as not only one of our more popular presidents, but also a competent one. He has charisma and brains. He will do whatever is in his power to keep our country great. When I watched his State-of-the Union message on television, I can't remember when I have been more proud to be an American, of the United States, or of my Commander-in-Chief; he made me so proud he brought tears to my eyes."

A LETTER TO PRESIDENT BUSH

Dear Mister President;

We want to draw your attention to some of the reasons *Colonel Maggie* (aka known as actress/entertainer Martha Raye) should be awarded the Presidential Medal of Freedom from you. If you'll read her story ... you have sufficient cause to award this medal. To help you with some background, please read over the following:

1. The 74th United States Congress, on June 29th, 1936, passed Private Law 727 awarding a gold Medal of Honor to George M. Cohan, the composer who wrote such songs as "*Over There*" and "*It's A Grand Old Flag*." It was the first time in history that Congress gave a medal to someone for writing "*songs*," but these songs were said to have "*inspired*" troops so greatly in a time of war.

2. In 1945, The Medal of Freedom was instituted by President Truman to recognize Americans "*who had made special meritorious contributions to world peace, the security or national interest of the United States or other public and private endeavors.*"

Some recipients include:

1983, Clare Booth Luce (diplomat/writer); James Burngham (historian).

1984, Anwar Sadat (Egyptian President); Howard H. Baker, Jr. (Senate Majority leader); James

Cagney (actor); Tennessee Ernie Ford (country singer); Louis L'Amour (writer); Reverend Norman Vincent Peale; Jackie Robinson (baseball player); Leo Cherne (economist); Dr. Denton Cooley (heart surgeon); General Andrew Goodpaster; Ballet Promoter, Lincoln Kirsten; Eunice Kennedy Shriver; Dr. Hector Garcia (founder of the Mexican-American Rights Group); and Ex-Soviet agent, Whittaker Chambers.

1988, the Presidential Medal of Freedom was given to Bob Hope; Sammy Davis, Jr.; Perry Como and Bette Davis, all entertainers.

1989, Polish Labor Leader Lech Walesa; heavyweight boxing champion, Joe Louis; Founder of NAACP, Clarence Mitchell; Danny Kaye; Meredith Wilson, and Judge Kaufman.

We veterans know of many of the recipients listed above and do not take it upon ourselves to judge but we do feel that our "*Old Lady of the Boondocks*" our "*Colonel Maggie*", our "*Sweetheart of Vietnam*" should, without doubt, be included in that group.

Most sincerely,

GI's from World War II, Korea, Vietnam

---

* And a special thanks to First Sergeant Mildred *Noonie* Fortin for her letter to Roy Benavidez including files and research material and especially for her efforts with the

Tri-County Council of Vietnam ERA Veterans for their pursuit in bringing the story of Martha Raye to the public. She tells us that Jimmy Dean, at the Special Forces Association, has collected 18,000 signatures on a petition to present to President Bush. It has taken him 8 years to get these signatures and only lack of publicity prevents him from collecting hundreds of thousands of names.

But, is all this necessary? Perhaps those of you who read this book will write to your congressman asking that *Maggie* be awarded her Medal of Freedom. She so justly deserves it.

General Patrick Cassidy presents Army Commendation Medal to Roy on July 10, 1972. Roy and the general were friends.

Daniel Castillo, Troop Commander, Class of 1982, at New Mexico Military Institute.

CAPTAIN DANIEL CASTILLO

Another individual I feel I should mention is a 28-year old Special Forces Captain named Danny Castillo. I accompanied Roy on a trip to San Antonio where Roy spoke to the graduating class of Special Forces medics at Brooke Army Medical Center. That evening, Danny's brother Benny picked us up at our motel and drove us to his house, where he and Danny live.

Danny heard of Roy Benavidez when he was a senior in high school in Denver City, Texas. He was so impressed with Roy's story - being a Green Beret, being Hispanic and being awarded the Medal of Honor - that Danny patterned his life to try and follow in Roy's footsteps. Roy was his role-model. This is what Danny wrote in his letter to me.

> "I couldn't believe Roy's story. The tremendous courage and conviction of duty just left me astounded. I was at a crossroads in life and needed something to give me commitment and the army seemed the place. It has discipline, it needs courageous people, and loyalty to others is respected. I wrote Roy a letter and three days later got a response. Who IS this man? I wondered. How can he be such a great hero yet take the time to write to me, a high school kid?
>
> "In October, 1985 I met Roy in Alabama at my Chemical Officer Basic Course Graduation ceremony. Roy was the guest speaker. When I heard his name I almost fainted. Here was Roy Benavidez, the nice man who has been answering letters from a kid he didn't even know, and he was here speaking at my graduation. I introduced myself, we hugged and patted each others back and my rolemodel now became my friend. He provided guidance to enhance my career.

"After graduation from high school at the New Mexico Military Institute, I received a B.S. degree from Angelo State and joined the Regular Army on active duty and completed several army schools. I was trained in Air Assault, U.S. Airborne, Honduran Airborne, Chilean Ranger-Commando, Special Forces Green Beret, Armor Tactical Training and as a Chemical Officer, my duty assignments included, Executive Officer and Company Commander of Alpha Company. 1st Battalion, 7th Special Forces Group and my duty stations were in Chile, South America and several classified missions on the Southern Border of the Republic of Honduras, Central America."

Danny was hit behind the neck by an enemy rifle butt while serving in Southern Honduras. His neck was broken. He was brought out of the jungles by medics and airlifted back to the United States suffering from pneumonia and in a coma. He wasn't expected to live.

After 4 1/2 weeks of intensive care at Brooke Army Medical Center in San Antonio, Texas, where he had a tracheotomy, Danny spent 2 1/2 months on a respirator then was sent to the V.A. Medical Center in Houston where he spent five months in traction.

Danny is married and has a 3-year old son. His wife applied for a divorce a few months ago. Danny doesn't blame her, he understands that *"for better or worse"* doesn't oftentimes mean that in a literal sense. He is a quadriplegic; he has only the limited use of his right hand. He is confined to a bed and has a 24-hour nurse. Much of the time his brother Benny is his nurse and has been at his side constantly.

Danny Castillo's life as he once knew it is over. He has hopes that some new contraption, some medical breakthrough, some miracle will happen to change it, but he is a survivor. He stays positive most of the time but there are times when it truly becomes a struggle. He has a bed that is mechanical and the limited use of his right hand allows him to dial a special telephone the V.A. has for him. He can control his TV and work his computer with amazing speed and accuracy and can feed himself some foods.

But, in order to move, he must be lifted from his bed to a motorized wheelchair, helped into a specially equipped van, and driven places. He has to be bathed and tended to constantly. He cannot walk through the park or run along a beach. He can't play football or baseball, go dancing, or jump from airplanes; but he is *alive*! He has survived and he is making the most of his life.

In our last conversation just a few days before Christmas he told me he got a job at his old alma mater, the *New Mexico State Military Institute*. He will be the assistant curator of their museum. Danny is so positive, so very brave, so resilient. He is truly a courageous young man who sacrificed his life to make our country a better place to live.

Those of you reading this book, take a few moments and write to Danny, will you? I know if you're military, he'd love hearing from you. And if not, he'd still love hearing from you.

        Capt. Daniel L. Castillo
        Assistant Museum Curator
        New Mexico Military Institute
        Rosewell, New Mexico 88201

The Green Beret friends meet again at Denver City, Texas for patriotic speech on October 19th, 1988.

JERRY COTTINGHAM

Roy gets letters from high school and grade school kids, from grandmothers, wives of servicemen who didn't make it back and from Special Forces comrades and other MOH recipients.

Just a few weeks ago Roy made a trip to Shreveport, Louisiana to visit Jerry Cottingham, the Special Forces sergeant who recognized and identified Roy as the medics were zipping him up in the body bag. Jerry was dying from cancer. When Roy learned of it, he got in his El Camino and drove the 600 miles to pay his last respects to his friend and fellow Green Beret.

Jerry died a few weeks after Roy's visit. I was with Roy when he heard the news. He became solemn, then excused himself after hanging up the telephone. When he returned, his face was freshly washed and I could tell he was disguising his emotions. Yes, real men shed tears too.

The day Jerry was buried Roy was addressing another group of young servicemen in Alabama. He mentioned Jerry and shared with them the story of how Jerry saved his life. And now, Jerry was gone.

Jerry Cottingham, a friend and hero.

Edward James Olmos and Roy on May 5th, 1987 (Cinco de Mayo - Mexican Independence Day), the day Roy was inducted into the Hispanic Hall of Fame. Roy hopes movie actor Olmos will play the starring role in an upcoming movie on Roy - Six Hours in Hell.

Mr. Olmos also gives talks to high schools, colleges, penal institutions, old-age homes, Indian reservations and hospitals. "Through discipline, we can get almost anywhere. There is an easy way and a hard way to do things. The hard way is to take the easy way, and the easy way is the hard way."

ISAAC GEORGE RODRIGUEZ

"Just today I received another telephone call from a relative in Houston," Roy said. "Their son was just killed in Panama."

Petty Officer 2nd Class Isaac George Rodriguez, III, age 24, a member of the navy SEAL team in Panama, had been killed in action while serving his country. The date, December 20th, 1989.

"Ikey" was buried in Houston National Cemetery on Veteran's Memorial Drive with traditional military honors. Roy attended his services at Notre Dame Church and at his burial. Monsignor William Pickard read the eulogy.

"Isaac was a young man who believed in responsibility. It was no surprise to me to learn that at 17, Isaac chose the form of service he knew had meaning for all in his own nation. Out of concern for his country and the people of Panama, he accepted his call to help with the ouster of Panamanian dictator/drug dealer General Manuel Noriega, who didn't allow freedom for his people."

At the funeral, Roy was interviewed by reporters. "Ikey always wanted to be a member of the SEALS, the elite fighting group of the Navy. It's horrible when you think about the fact that many people spent a lifetime in the service. I spent 25 years of my life, a lot of it in combat, and Ikey gets killed his *first day* in combat. It doesn't seem fair. In the Green Berets or SEALS, only God knows our love for our fellow man and country."

Petty Officer 2nd Class Rodriguez was assigned to disable Noriega's private jet and attempt to capture him on the morning of December 20th, 1989. A Navy SEAL at the funeral who participated in the assault told Roy, "*Ikey went back to get a wounded comrade. He got killed doing it.*" That comrade is one of the wounded recuperating at the Brooke Army Medical Center in San Antonio.

* Noriega has since turned himself over to the United States Drug Enforcement Agency. He prefers being charged for drug trafficking in the US rather than by the people of Panama who want him for drugs, brutality to a nation, and murder! Noriega is now incarcerated in a Florida prison.

Roy believes so devoutly in America that he often gives his speeches with "fire and brimstone" rhetoric. At NASA in 1989, he addressed a group of several hundred honoring National Hispanic Month. He begins his talks with a standing ovation and leaves with one.

BARRY SADLER

I think every veteran alive has heard of Barry Sadler, who along with author, Robin Moore, wrote *The Ballad of the Green Berets*, which sold a reported 9 million singles and albums. Not to mention him in this text would be remiss on my part.

Sadler served one tour of duty in the Air Force before enlisting in the Army and volunteering for Special Forces. He became a member of SF in early 1963 and graduated as a SF medic in March of '64. He was assigned to Company A, 7th Special Forces Group, as an A-Team medic. When he reenlisted for 3 years he was then assigned to Headquarters Company, 3rd Special Forces Group, as the senior medical specialist in the group surgeon's office.

In August of 1964 he deployed to Vietnam for duty with Company C of the 5th Special Forces Group in the Central Highlands as A-Team medic and was later evacuated for a wound sustained by a punji stake while on patrol. He returned to Fort Bragg as the senior medical specialist in the JFK Special Warfare surgeon's office and was still recovering from his knee wound when he wrote and recorded his famous song.

After leaving the service, he appeared in at least one motion picture and began to write a series of books using a military theme that have been published in millions of copies.

On November 5th, 1989, Barry Allen Sadler died. He was hospitalized in the Alvin C. York Medical Center in Tennessee at the time of his death and had been undergoing treatment for brain damage suffered from a gunshot wound in Guatemala in 1988.

He is survived by his wife, Lavona; two sons; Thor and Baron; a daughter, Brooke; and a brother, Robert.

Vietnamese "Killer Cowboy" fighting for our side.

POW Camp in Vietnam, holding NVA and Viet Cong.

"MAD DOG" SHRIVER

One of the most colorful, patriotic, soldiers to ever fight for the United States in *any* war, was a Sergeant First Class in the U.S. Army named Jerry M. "*Mad Dog*" Shriver. Veterans around the world either know him or know "of" him because his appetite for combat was legendary. He was so "gung ho" that they couldn't keep him out of the field. One day his commander issued a direct order to *Mad Dog* to take some R & R in Saigon or Da Nang, wherever he pleased. A few days passed and this commander was visiting an forward operating base in Viet Nam when an extraction slick came in. The commander went to the airstrip and discovered *Mad Dog* as part of that extraction team. Shriver's idea of having fun was to run missions in a new area.

Over the years, *Mad Dog* Shriver's exploits became so legendary that *Radio Hanoi* began taunting him. The story has it that *Mad Dog* became so irate that he often switched his radio frequency to the Communist channels, and either told them where he was going next to see if they would like to try and stop him, or issued someone or another a personal challenge.

Mad Dog was part of a reenforced platoon of several Special Forces troopers and twenty-five Montagnards in late April of 1969. The SOG group, all hardened and experienced fighters, scrambled for cover when they met with a withering barrage of machine gun fire from the North Vietnamese. Shriver got up and led a commando charge into the machine gun fire and disappeared into the trees. The team called for extraction. The team leader was temporarily blinded, his assistant team leader and medic killed, and the platoon all but wiped out. It took over 2000 rockets, ten air strikes and napalm to cover the extraction slicks who took out the remaining team members.

Shriver was nowhere to be found. The army declared him MIA. Those who knew *Mad Dog* are certain he survived. They feel he made it through that wall of NVA and into the safety of the jungles where he is "probably working for the CIA performing a mission we don't know about." Many SOG veterans feel *Mad Dog* finally "bought the farm."

Here is a photo of *Mad Dog* in his heyday. He was a young man who was proud of his country. He felt he was needed to help the US win the war in Vietnam, never realizing that we never lost it; we just weren't given permission to win it.

Master Sergeant Jerry M. "Mad Dog" Shriver ready for recon patrol. He was reported MIA after fierce firefight on April 24th, 1969. There is no confirmation on his death or whereabouts.

PART V

WRAPPING IT UP

YOUNG AMERICANS

Of all the groups Roy appears before, he seems to prefer the school kids most of all.

"I travel most of the time - everywhere. I am greeted by Hispanics and Anglos and just *people*. What warms my heart most is when I visit these schools and see these youngster, black, white, brown and recently, many Asians. These kids are growing up in a complex world, but one that is more accepting than the world I grew up in. Certainly there is still prejudice and racism scattered here and there, but it is changing; it's changing for the good. These kids ask me questions about war, about the military, even about being a Hispanic, and they listen. They seem to understand that prejudice and racism will soon, hopefully, be found only in history books. Most of these young people aren't aware of prejudice. It's their *parents* who need schooling.

"When I say it's '*the parent's who need schooling*' I must explain that I don't mean to act like a know-it-all because, the Lord knows, I certainly have a lot to learn myself. My wife, Lala, raised my three. I was their father and I provided for them the best I could and tried to set an example for them too and I certainly don't have all the answers. But parents need to get closer to their children and must constantly *monitor* their child's actions and be aware of the pitfalls: drugs, alcohol, sex, cults even. They must watch them in grade school and through high school. No matter how big a youngster gets, they are the direct responsibility of the parents until they leave the roost. Even afterwards.

"Kids usually follow what they are taught at home. If the parents fight and argue, it makes for an unhappy child. If the parents use illegal drugs around the house, of course the kids feel they can use drugs. If the parents are racists, why wouldn't the child absorb at least some of this stupidity? If the parents aren't aware of the effects and signs of various drugs, they had best get schooling *fast*! You see it every day and if you're not out in the world witnessing these things, turn on the television and watch Geraldo, Sally Jessy Raphel, Oprah, or Donahue and listen to some of their guests who were unaware of what their children were doing until it was too late.

"There are some wonderful young people out there; I see hundreds of them each week on my speaking tour. These kids listen to me, it seems, more than they listen to their parents. I have no direct bond with them, you know, no reason to tell them things to make my life easier...no personal or selfish motives. So, these young people listen to what I say. And when I show up in full dress uniform, I know that impresses the kids. But I'd show up in a *clown costume* if it made them listen.

"I tell these children and young adults about the evils of drugs. I beg them to continue their education and be somebody. I ask them to get along with each other and to pay attention to their parents and teachers. And, of course, I tell them about loving America - their country. I explain to them that they can become whatever they want to be regardless of their race, religion, background, or financial level. With the belief in God, with being willing to try, they too can become important.

School children pledge allegiance to our flag before listening to Roy.

Roy visits shelter for "runaways" in Hutchinson, Kansas.

A visit with West Point Military Academy cadets.

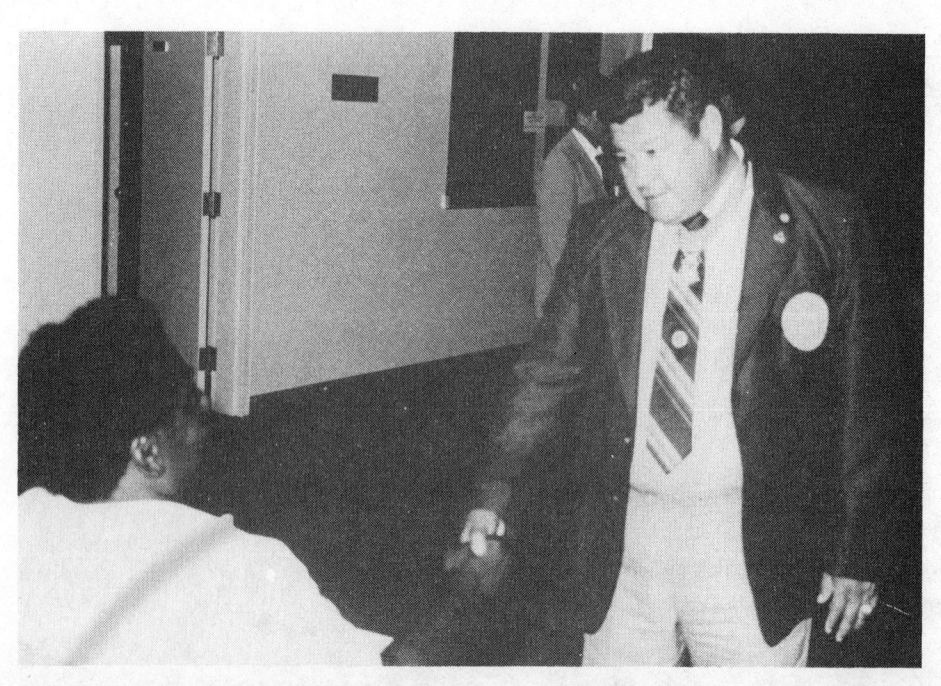

VA hospital patients welcome him.

I went through several huge boxes of letters Roy received from kids during the past several years. I chose some to share with you.

Dear Sergeant Benavidez;

I just finished reading a story about you and I just wanted you to know that it gave me a different look at life, see I'm sixteen years old and My father is stationed in Korea. And I'm Kind of worried about him over there. I live with My Mom Now at fort McAllen AL. Your story has given me the faith and determination to make it through some lonely Nights. Congratulations on winning the Medal of Honor. Thank You and God bless! Your friend.

* Young man who missed his dad.

Dear Roy;

Hello! How are you? Fine I hope. The reason I am Writing is because I'ma big fan of yours. I think it's great that you got the congressional Medal of Honor. That's wonderful!

Could I please have an autographed photo of you? It would mean a lot to me. Thank you so much! You are a real inspiration. God Bless you.

* Letter from a 7th grader at Ortega Junior High school.

FOR HIS COUNTRY'S HONOR

A man who leaves his family willingly to fight for his country's honor, should be honored for that deed. And a man who shows great bravery, courage, and intelligence in times of battle; should be given his country's most distinguished award.

And here today we are honored to be in the presence of MSG. ROY P. BENAVIDEZ. He is a man who fought in such a special way for his country's honor, that he was given the most distinguished award; the Congressional Medal of Honor.

And certainly whoever receives an award such as this, like Sgt. Benavidez did, is a person to be looked upon as an example of today and tomorrow's way.

* This tribute was written to Roy from a ninth grader at Edinburgh Jr. High School.

Hundreds of school children hear Roy say, "Learn - then use what you learn."

LETTERS TO ROY

FROM: Vice-President of the United States, George Bush.

Dear Roy;   May 19, 1987

Congratulations on your recent induction into the Hispanic Hall of Fame. I know you to be richly deserving of this national recognition, both for your important contributions to the Hispanic community and to our great country. Well done, my friend.

Warmest regards,

George Bush

P.S. Your letter of May 13 just hit my desk. You make us all proud! I'll give Barbara your message, and we both hope to see you soon.

FROM: President of the United States, Ronald Reagan. The White House, January 20, 1987

Dear Sergeant Benavidez;

Donna Alvarado has forwarded the copy of your book bearing your warm inscription. Your kindness in sharing it with me is truly appreciated. Please know I am proud to have your life-story as a special reminder of your friendship. With my very best wishes to you and your family.

Sincerely,

Ronald Reagan

FROM: Carl W. Griffin, CSM, U.S. Army (Ret)

"Needless to say, I am proud of you, and proud to have been part of a great fraternity. As you know, it was from the best we had to offer that the Special Forces were born in the late fifties, and a new era. You are a part of that legend, Roy, one of the true heroes. You take your place in history along with the other great men and battle units."

Carl W. Griffin, CSM, U.S. Army (Ret)

FROM: Department of The Air Force
Elmendorf Air Force Base, Alaska

"The men and women of the 21st Tactical Fighter Wing were honored to have you as our guest speaker at Elmendorf AFB during National Hispanic Heritage Week. Your participation during this special observance reemphasized that Hispanic people are an integral part of our military services and full participants in all facets of American life. Your commitment to "Duty, Honor, Country" has strengthened the military and its standards."

"Our Hispanic people's traditions, language and culture are a vital part of our American heritage. They have always been served in the Armed Forces of our great nation with dedication and distinction. Their strong devotion to family, deep religious convictions, and pride in their heritage help make America a better place to live."

"We are all so very proud of you, Master Sergeant Benavidez. We were privileged to have a Medal of Honor recipient with us but equally proud of what you are doing after your time in the service and how you serve as a role-model to our youth of today."

*Department of The Air Force
Elmendorf Air Force Base, Alaska*

FROM: Lieutenant General Dave R. Palmer, USA
Superintendent, West Point

"The conference room that will bear your name will serve to remind future cadets that the sacrifices of soldiers have made and kept our country great."

FROM: Cadet Cynthia Ramirez at West Point

"Thank your for your commitment and dedication to our country. You are a real inspiration. God bless you."

FROM: Rudy Abramson, Los Angeles Times
Washington Bureau

"I took my 10-year old daughter with me to the Pentagon. When we entered the Hall of Heroes I showed her your plaque and told her about you. She was impressed and, of course, could understand a story of one person much better than she could grasp

the real meaning of the plaques from all the wars. You are her hero."

FROM: Charlie Thop, President
      Rotary Club of Houston Heights
      Houston, Texas

"It has been a long time, if ever, that I have been as moved as I was with any speaker. You shamed me. Sergeant Benavidez, and made me feel how frightened I was of war or of the chance of dying. When in May 1968, you were fighting for your life and country, I was fighting for peace on a campus because I felt the war was wrong! I had two cousins who fought in Vietnam, one a Blue Beret (instructor) and one a naval fighter pilot. But neither one made me see the war and feel it in the way you expressed it."

"You said that anyone would have done what you did to save your fellow comrades. I can't say that I would have had the nerve to do what you did. But what you did made me more proud that I have been in a long time to be an American."

"I salute you and all other Americans who fought for America. Thank you for giving me the chance to meet you."

FROM: Margaret Ann Westphall to Chris Barbee

"Dear Chris Barbee; Please print this article I wrote for the YUMA DAILY SUN in your newspaper. It's

about a friend of yours, Roy Benavidez. I think about him from time to time. I am still in awe. Meeting him really heightened my respect for ALL veterans."

The article:

"Editor, The Sun: I would like to share with you and your readers one of the most beautiful experiences of my life. Sgt. Roy Benavidez was seated next to me enroute from Phoenix to Yuma on September 16th (1981). We had 50 minutes to talk, and in those 50 minutes he told me more about humanity, humility, and heroes that I'll ever hear for years to come. But then, Congressional Medals of Honor are not bestowed on ordinary human beings."

"The media is limited only to the highlights, the hoopla and the hallelujah given to our heroes. Heroes are far more complicated than newspapers and TV have time for them to be, so allow me to fill in a few spaces."

"Sgt. Benavidez is probably one of the most humble people I've ever met. He's basically shy, and a little embarrassed by the fuss...but you will never in your life meet a man who is more turned on by America and its youth. You will never meet a man who has given so much to defend America. The man is covered with scars...he pointed to one and said, 'I have to see a doctor in Yuma about this (a large piece of shrapnel I could feel and see, that was working its way out of his arm).' All I could think of was that he got it for me. And mine. And yours."

"He was awarded FIVE purple hearts, but he wears only one with two Oak leaf clusters. He was wearing his uniform that day; he was on his way to speak to young children at several local schools in Yuma. He feels heroes ought to set an example for the young ones and his uniform gets their attention. I hope my young one is influenced by this man."

"I spent four years as a flight attendant with an airline that carried wounded soldiers from Vietnam. I met a lot of heroes at that time. I saw many of them come home in the belly of my airplane in flag-draped coffins. Thank God this one got back alive to spread the word...America and its people are a wonderful lot. You have his word on it."

"Sgt. Benavidez still hurts a lot, from the injuries both physical and mental. I felt so proud sitting next to him, talking with him, watching him, and listening to what he felt about his country, the youth of today, and the future of America. I felt so proud that I shook his hand several times and gave him a kiss on the cheek. I only wish I had a band."

West Point Cadet
Cynthia Ramirez, class of '90.

WALTER KRUGER is President of the NCOA (Non Commissioned Officers Association of the United States of America), a fraternal, non-profit organization which provides multiple services for the non-coms from all branches of the service. He has held that position since being elected in 1984. He was reelected in 1987 and will probably serve again from 1990 or until he decides to retire. The two projects Mr. Kruger is high on are, the Scholarship Fund and the NCOA Medical Trust Fund.

WALTER KRUGER, competent, affable, combat veteran, heads the NCOA.

* The SCHOLARSHIP FUND is for children and spouses of members of the NCOA, for study at accredited colleges, universities, and vocational training institutes. Over $500,000 has been donated to the scholarship fund since its inception.

* The NCOA Medical Trust Fund, originally established in 1983, provides financial assistance to military personnel to alleviate incidental expenses incurred as a result of a major medical procedure of a member of their immediate family. Assistance my be provided as non-repayable grants or in the form of no-interest loans.

* In 1990, the NCOA presented the Roy P. Benavidez Leadership award to the Special Operations Medical Sergeants Course. The first recipient of this award was Staff Sergeant Sucel P. Delacruz, shown here receiving the plaque from the hero it was named after.

ROY'S AWARDS AND DECORATIONS

1. Congressional Medal of Honor

2. Purple Heart with FOUR Oak leaf Clusters (each cluster signifies a multiple award)

3. Meritorious Service Medal

4. Army Commendation Medal

5. Army Achievement Medal

6. Good Conduct Medal (with 5 loops, each loop represents 5 years of good conduct)

7. Army of Occupation Medal (Berlin)

8. National Defense Service Medal with one Oak leaf Cluster

9. Armed Forces Expeditionary Medal

10. Vietnam Service Medal with 4 campaign stars

11. NCO Professional Development Ribbon

12. Army Service Ribbon

13. Overseas Service Ribbon

14. United Nations Service Medal

15. Republic of Vietnam Campaign Medal

16. Presidential Unit Citation with 2 Oak leaf Clusters

17. Meritorious Unit Commendation Ribbon

18. Republic of Vietnam Cross of Gallantry with Palm Unit Citation

19. Republic of Vietnam Civil Action Unit Citation with Palm

20. Combat Infantry Badge

21. Master Parachute Badge

22. Vietnamese Jump Wings

Even generals are in awe of the Medal of Honor. General Willie Scott, former Adjutant General of State of Texas, gets closer look at MOH.

HONORS

1. Roy Benavidez has received keys and honorary mayorship to several US cities.

2. The "Roy P. Benavidez Airborne Museum" at the Battleship Texas anchored near Houston.

3. ROTC Honor Saber at Southwest Texas State University.

4. Edinburg High School JROTC Drill Team named in his honor.

5. Roy Benavidez exhibit at the Wharton County Historical Museum.

6. Saber from West Point given to him at a Retreat Ceremony when the entire West Point Core of Cadets marched in review.

7. El Campo, Texas National Guard Armory named in his honor.

8. U.S. Naval Reserve Training Center of three and a half million compliment named in his honor.

9. Over 300 magazines and newspapers have recorded his war record, combat record, and the personal speeches he's given all over the United States.

10. Roy's most recent honor was being named in WHO'S WHO among Hispanic-Americans.

There are many more honors, far too numerous to list. He is, however, a LIFE MEMBER of the American Legion, Post #76 in Austin, Texas. A member of the V.F.W. Post in Wooster, Ohio; DAV Post 72 in El Campo, Texas; American GI Forum; LULAC's S.F. (Decade) Association; 82nd Airborne Association; 11th Airborne Association; Vietnam Veterans Brotherhood Association; Life member of the NCOA.

General William Westmoreland, Chief of Staff of the U.S. Army, visits with his former driver. Not even generals rate a Medal of Honor recipient as a driver. They share extreme pride of each other.

EPILOG

Roy Benavidez still lives in El Campo, Texas and travels several times a week to make speeches to schools, civic, and business organizations and to open or commemorate or dedicate something or other.

When the weather changes and gets cold-even cool-the multiple wounds, the torn muscles and ligaments, and the mounds of scar tissue cause him pain. He keeps his positive attitude, his marvelous sense of humor, and he makes time to help others.

He was concerned over hearing one day that *"Hispanic people don't stick together anymore,"* and this bothered him greatly. He doesn't believe it. And as far as the heroes of the Hispanics, his friend and mine, Chris Gomez, a Special Forces soldier who lives in Chicago told us, *"Hispanics are a proud people. It's the Indian blood that flows through our veins. We're proud and we give our life for our country without a second thought. More Hispanics received the Medal of Honor During World War II than all other ethnic groups put together. We are proud of our country and we will fight for it until the death."*

Roy, of course, feels the same way. He has so many friends (and relatives) from all over the country. He and his friend, Ab Webber, were in Los Angeles a few years ago at a large gathering of West Pointers to see the Army/Navy football game. Their hotel was sort of in the *boonies*, and there were no cabs available to take them to football game on the opposite end of the city.

Roy used the telephone directory and made a few calls. Within the hour, no less than *eight* large, black limousines arrive to load Roy, Ab and *forty-eight* family members and West Point classmate in those limos normally used for funerals. Roy, it seems, has a cousin who is with the police force who had a friend (*Trevino Funeral Home*) who took them on the 60-mile trek to the stadium, accompanied them to the ball game and drove them back. Mr. Trevino has yet to send the bill Ab asked him to send.

I went with Roy to the MOH dinner in Chicago in August, 1989. At the airport we were picked up by four of his friends in yet another limo. These four Hispanics, none wealthy, pooled their money to rent this fine car to pick up their friend from Texas. They love Roy, and they respect him, and they accepted me even *before* they learned that my mother's maiden name was Hernandez. But they went too far. Some way or other I was *caught* with four of them at about 3 a.m. in some desolate section of Chicago. They drove us in a Mercedes, borrowed from the cousin of one of the guys in the car.

We ended up on a street that was wide awake; lights, restaurants, and clubs open and lots of people. I follow this unholy troop into a restaurant where everyone was speaking Spanish. I knew maybe fifty words and, of course, can't understand a thing they are saying. They all order the specialty of the house, *Menudo*. I ordered Guacomole and chips. When the food is served, I watched Roy take a few *handfuls* of ground black pepper, at least one minute of squirts from a *Tabasco* bottle, a salad plate brimming with raw onion...and dump it into this large bowl of Menudo. I couldn't resist. I had to taste it.

One *sip* and my eyes sprung water like a sprinkler. I didn't cough; I was strangling. I didn't have a fire in my mouth, I had a fire *truck* in it and it was *on* fire! Anyway, I learned of Menudo. I might try in again but maybe just straight, not with all the *fixins'*.

Roy Benavidez is my friend; I love the guy. He has a terrific sense of humor and his outlook is always positive. He believes in the American flag and what it stands for.

His commander in chief, whoever it might be through the years, is one he will listen to and obey regardless of what he is asked to do, Roy knowing he would not be asked to do anything that would harm his fellow-man or country.

You might meet someone *as* patriotic as Roy, but nobody *more* patriotic. He was so special in war and he is equally as special in peace. As he travels around the world showing the underprivileged that they can succeed, as he gives his talks to young people everywhere, as he address business and veterans groups and makes appearance at grade schools, high schools, colleges, and universities, they will all hear the three words he lives by:

DUTY - HONOR - COUNTRY.

His audiences *all* stand and applaud when he finishes a speech, and most have tears in their eyes. This man is one special human being. He is a patriot, a husband, father, and a friend to all. I am so very proud to have the honor to write some things about him and to spend the time with him while doing my research. I care for him so much that if I visit him at dinner time, and he is serving Menudo...unless he personally adds those extras to it...I'll sit with him and enjoy it.

The young Roy Benavidez picked cotton in West Texas fields. At 14, he was a 7th grade school dropout.

Roy became a combat soldier.

EPILOG

And now, the recipient of the MEDAL OF HONOR where his portrait hangs in the Hall of Heroes in the Pentagon. "You can be whatever you want to be if you learn...and if you try."

"AIRBORNE ALL THE WAY"   Sicily drop zone at Fort Bragg.

WRAPPING IT UP

"The story I've told you is true, every word. Nothing has been added, deleted, or embellished. It is my story and I want to tell it the way it actually was even though it might offend someone. I hope it does, because the pain, the horror of war, the bloodshed and loss of life should be offensive to everyone. As long as there are human beings who disagree, there will be war. The very killing in war is a mortal sin. But to allow some of the atrocities inflicted on some by others simply must be stopped. If the only way to stop this heinous treatment to innocents by others is war, and - woefully so - it oftentimes is, then I shall go to war. Yes, I apologize for some humans but not for humanity."

MSG. (Ret) Roy P. Benavidez

Combat Veteran - Proud American

Roy meets with President Reagan again. MOH recipient Rudy Hernandez smiles in the background.

Highly acclaimed radio talk-show host, Bernard Wishnow, (Mr. Wish) hosting Roy and author, Pete Billac on KSEV radio in Houston.

BIBLIOGRAPHY

ABOVE AND BEYOND... perhaps *the* most inspirational book I read while doing research. It is, "A History of the Medal of Honor from the Civil War to Vietnam." There are wonderful, adventurous, thrilling, and heart-rending stories, a complete history of the medal, recipients of the medal, and lots of photographs. It is published by Boston Publishing Company and lists several qualified and competent writers. I've seen it in libraries and many bookstores. If you want it and can't find it, order it through your nearest bookstore. It is a *must* book for the veteran or historian and excellent reading for the young as well as the not-so-young.

THE CONGRESSIONAL MEDAL OF HONOR...The names and the deeds, published by Sharp and Dunnigan.

THE GREEN BERETS... written by Robin Moore, published by Crown.

VIETNAM MEDAL OF HONOR HEROES...by Edward Murphy, an Army veteran of the Vietnam War who served one year as president of the Medal of Honor Historical Society. Published by Ballentine Books.

HEROES...written by Alexander Jason. The true account of the Medal of Honor winners (recipients), Southeast Asia, 1964-1975, published by The Anite Press.

INSIDE THE GREEN BERETS...written by Charles M. Simpson, III, published by Presidio. This book tells of the *First Thirty Years*, a history of the U.S. Army Special Forces. Simpson is a colonel (retired) who spent 30 years in the Army, nine years with Special Forces. A terrific book that tells you "inside" information found in few other books.

NAM...written by Mark Baker and published by Berkley in paperback. A national bestseller. The Vietnam War in the words of the soldiers who fought there.

AMONG THE VALIANT...by Raul Morin and published by Borden Publishing. It highlights the valor of Mexican-Americans in World War II and Korea.

VIETNAM - ORDER OF BATTLE...author, Shelby L. Stanton, a complete, illustrated reference to the U.S. Army and Allied Ground Forces in Vietnam, 1961-1973. This book also was in Roy's personal library with an inscription from Captain Stanton, "with warmest personal regards to a true Vietnam hero and fellow Special Forces comrade." Shelby Stanton, Captain, (retired) served for six years as an infantry officer with the 3rd Brigade of the 82nd Airborne Division, 5th Special Forces Group, 20th Combat Engineer Brigade and as an Airborne Ranger Special Forces advisor. He was highly decorated during his military service.

THE HISTORY OF THE VIETNAM WAR...by Charles T. Kamps, Jr., Chris Bishop, Ian C. Drury and David K. Donald. A marvelous book with more than 700 color and black and white photographs and illustrations. Talks of Green Berets, Seals, chopper pilots, tunnel rats, marines, Delta Force, Air Force, and River Patrol Boats. Published by The Military Press and distributed by Crown Publishers.

THE KILLING ZONE...by Frederick Downs and published by Berkley Books in paperback. The *Baltimore News-American* called it, "*Human drama and frighteningly reality*

BIBLIOGRAPHY

...ranks with the best of the literature on the war."

AND...the following newspapers and magazines: *Austin-American Statesman; Houston Post; Los Angles Times; Washington Post; New York Times; Houston Chronicle; Yuma Daily-Sun and, the El Campo Leader-News.* Valor; Hispanic Magazine; Military; El Hispano News; NCOA Journal; Army Times; The Catholic War Veteran; Vista; The Veteran Leader; The National Amvet; The Smoking Gun; DAV Magazine; The American Legion; Texas VVA News;

PHOTO CREDITS TO:

BUDDDY GEE, Public Affairs Officer at Fort Sam Houston.

RAF HABEEB, executive with the NCOA in San Antonio, Texas.

DICK BISHOP, editor of The Drop, S.F. magazine at Fort Bragg, North Carolina.

WADE McMACKINS, for his action photographs.

ROGER WAGGIE, who made dozens of telephone calls, and as many letters, and loaned several personal photos. Roger also helped fill in some gaps about that day on May 2nd, 1968 and to correct my terminology on helicopters.

CHARLES GARZA for A0723-90-01822 FSHTX, SOMED Roy Benavidez Leadership award.

BOB O'BRIEN, Executive Director of the Illinois Vietnam Veterans Leadership Program for inviting me (the author) to be his guest and accompany Roy to Chicago for the Annual MOH Convention. Meeting these other MOH recipients gave me more understanding and aided me greatly in being able to tell about Roy. Also, for his clearance on the cover photo.

CENTRAL PHOTO FACILITY, Ft. Sam Houston, Texas, for U.S. Army Photograph by Salinas.

PUBLIC INFORMATION DIVISION, Office of the Chief of Information and Education, Department of the Army, Pentagon, Washington 25, DC for US Army photographs, #'s 41-133-5131-1/AK-68; 41-133-5337-1/AF-76; A0723-90-01822; 41-133-3821-2/AK-72.

J.F.K. SPECIAL WARFARE MUSEUM at Fort Bragg, North Carolina.

SP-4 RYLES for West Point photos; USMA-C-3172/AH81 and SP-5 Hordeski for USMA-C-3008/AH81.

DAVE VALDEZ, photographer for White House photos.

CHRIS BARBEE, photographs and story.

LALO HERNANDEZ, for his many photographs.

BIBLIOGRAPHY

SPECIAL THANKS TO:

FRED BARBEE, for his story on Roy. Because of the depth and quality of Mr. Barbee's story, it was copied by newspapers around the world and was the catalyst for a series of events that ultimately brought Roy his Medal of Honor. He is also one of Roy's most treasured friends.

CHRIS BARBEE, Fred's son, who has been a friend of Roy Benavidez for many years and who has aided Roy in so many ways. Chris is managing editor of the *EL CAMPO LEADER-NEWS* and helped with facts and letters for this book. *"Chris knows more about me than I do,"* Roy says with a smile.

RICHARD CAVAZOS, a four-star general (retired) who also gave Roy guidance through his term in the military. He suggested various schools and urged Roy to attend. They met several times during their military careers and the general took a liking to the young soldier. In 1966, then a Lieutenant Colonel serving as a battalion commander in the 1st Division (the Big Red 1) Richard Cavazos and Roy met again at a Special Forces camp in Vietnam.

BILL DARLING - *Why* wasn't he awarded a Medal of Honor? Or at least a DSC for his part in that rescue. He volunteered, he faced almost certain death, he fought heroically, and he was wounded. There were many heroes who were never recognized. But Roy knows he owes his life to many people, with Warrant Officer Bill Darling's name near the top of the list.

RALPH DRAKE, Lieutenant Colonel US Army (Ret), former commander of B-56, for recommending Roy for the MOH. Once Colonel Drake had gathered all the information concerning that mission on May 2nd, 1968, he began an arduous pursuit to see that Roy was recognized for his valor in volunteering and for recovering classified documents.

LEO FOISNER, Roy's favorite cousin, for being a true friend to Roy throughout the years. Leo was present at a talk I (the author) gave and immediately told Roy, "You've got to meet this guy. He will write your best-seller for you."

LEONEL M. GARZA, Assistant Superintendent for Finance and Support Services for the El Campo Independent School District. He is the past principal of El Campo High School and has been Roy's friend for over two decades. Mr. Garza helped Roy in making speeches, especially with the words *of the young* so Roy could reach these students while giving a talk to them. He assisted in Roy's education and urged Roy to continue his education by going to college after the military. He is a special person in Roy's life and Roy asked that he be thanked publicly.

LALO HERNANDEZ, MSgt. (Retired) from the U.S. Army in Special Forces, was an instructor in Special Forces training at Fort Bragg. He and his wife, Gloria, are godparents of Denise, Roy's lovely daughter. Sergeant Hernandez took special interest in Roy during training and admired the guts and perseverance in the young, soon-to-be, Green Beret.

JERRY (SKI) LEDZINSKY, B-56 teammate of Roy. Then-Captain Ledzinsky, *"Dai-uy"*, (Vietnamese for captain) was a fine combat soldier, a much revered leader, and a captain of Strike Force teams. Roy speaks often of Ski and mentions him in his prayers. *"Some of what Ski endured was too strong for most men. I hope he realizes the duty he performed, the many lives he saved, and how he helped our country free the world of communism."*

BRIAN O'CONNOR, the man *most* responsible for this book. Had Brian not read Fred Barbee's story and come forth to write that 8-page letter to President Reagan, Roy would never have been recognized for the Medal of Honor. Brian was the only eyewitness alive who could be used to testify for Roy. As the author of this book, Brian's input was invaluable. As Roy's comrade-in-arms, Brian will always remain special to Roy.

ROBIN TORNOW, Brigadier General, USAF, for his gallant support in the recovery of the team on May 2nd, 1968, and for information given to Roy that enabled the author to piece facts and action to make this book become reality. And to the Air Force support pilots for their efforts to save the entire team. Without the valorous actions and support of all these people, Roy would not be alive.

AB WEBBER, investor, entrepreneur, West Point graduate and true patriot; a friend to Roy for many years. Ab is a member of the Board of Trustees at West Point and is CEO of several major corporations. Roy has admiration and love for Ab and his mother, Margie.

GENE BUCKEL, investor in oil and real estate, boyhood friend of the author. "Gene was one of the finest high school athletes in Louisiana history, who has helped enormously in the production of this book. His son, Bart, is at LSU and plans on the military as his career."

GLOSSARY

This glossary is for those who have not been in the military or served in combat. You will gain a better understanding of terms used in this book or those you hear in motion pictures. Military terms are numbers, letters, a combination of both, or slang terms for various pieces of equipment, people or situations and no one can generally pinpoint their origins. If some GI says something that sounds cute, descriptive, or short, it makes for faster communication. Military jargon usually distinguishes someone who has served in the military from someone who hasn't.

AK-47 - Russian-made assault rifle normally used by the North Vietnamese and Viet Cong. It fires a 7.62 mm bullet from a 30-round clip and weighs a bit over 11 pounds, loaded. It is rated as one of the most successful and widely-used of any type of small arm ever produced. The designer was Mikhail Kalashnikov. It is a semi or fully-automatic weapon.

APC - Armored Personnel Carrier on tracks.

ARVN - Army of the Republic of Vietnam was rebuilt with the assistance of the US advisors between 1957 and 1959.

ATL - Assistant Team Leader. Each SF group has a TL (team leader) and an second in command called the ATL.

BASE CAMP - A permanent base of operations. The Special Forces had SF such camps spread throughout South Vietnam.

BEEHIVE ROUNDS - An explosive artillery shell which delivers thousands of small projectiles, *like nails with fins*, instead of shrapnel.

BIRD DOG - Term used for small (25' length, total weight under 1,500 pounds with 100 pound payload - safe weight after pilot and fuel) fixed-wing, single-seat aircraft with a small engine that would fly across battle zones and report back to base with information on troop movement or radio transmissions.

BLOOD TRAIL - A trail of blood left by someone wounded and bleeding.

BOUNCING BETTY - A mine that flies out of the ground when you step on it. A springlike trigger is released and it *bounces* about waist high and explodes spouting shards of metal designed to kill or disable.

BUSH HAT - Soft, cloth, camouflaged hat with a soft brim worn by Special Forces.

BUSTING CAPS - Slang for firing a weapon. The reference is probably some soldiers idea of shooting caps from a toy pistol. Once said, these slang terms often became normal talk. Further signified that a veteran was talking, not a Cherry.

C & C - Command and Control. A pilot who flys his chopper above, over and through a battle area, usually at 3000 to 5000 feet so he can see what is happening to ground troops. He reports back to headquarters and keeps in radio and visual contact with those on the ground. He radios for air strikes, calls in artillery as well as directs extraction helicopters to a PZ.

CHERRY - Slang term for a new recruit, not battle-tested.

CHINOOK - A large transport helicopter powered by two rotors and shaped like a bread box with a rotor at each end. Carries heavy artillery or as many as 44 men. Can carry over 10,000 lbs. (Model changes differ in payload)

CHOPPER - A name called most helicopters. A "chopper" could be a gunship, heavy equipment helicopter or a transport helicopter. We'll get into other "chopper" terminology with words like *gunship* or *slick* as we progress with these descriptions.

CHU HOI - *I surrender* in Vietnamese. Not a literal translation but it was understood by both sides.

C-4 - An explosive material called plastique. Many GI's in the jungles used shavings from C-4 to start a fire. It burned like Sterno and was used to warm coffee or as a smoke signal.

CIDG - Civilian Independent Defense Group, made up of South Vietnamese who volunteer to fight to defend their village and country. The US trained these combat soldiers and many worked with Special Forces teams to aid as interpreters, trackers, and combatants.

CLAYMORE - A fragmentation, antipersonnel mine that sends a swarth in an arc-shaped pattern to its front. In large letters on claymore, it reads *FRONT*, fool-proof so it will not be turned the wrong way.

CO - Commanding Officer, lovingly (but not outwardly) referred to as the *Old Man*. Some of these *old men* - platoon leaders - were barely twenty. Usually the CO was a battalion (maybe company) commander.

COBRA - An Army helicopter, armed with a 40 mm grenade launcher and a 6-barrel (Gatling) machine gun in the nose turret. There are pods for 52 rockets and often with extra miniguns installed on the inboard pylons. On the AH-Cobra, the gunner was in the forward cockpit. Usually marked with shark's mouth design; white sharp teeth printed over a red mouth. Frightening and lethal.

CONCERTINA WIRE - Barbed wire that is rolled out along the ground to prevent or impede the progress of ground troops. If you watch movies on war you will see this wire in large rolls stretched around the perimeter of a base camp.

CP - Command post.

DMZ - Demilitarized Zone.

DONUT DOLLIE - Name given to Red Cross girls who hand out coffee and donuts. These Red Cross volunteers were always a welcome sight to any GI and the name, though not a provocative one, was given in respect, friendship, and appreciation.

DUSTOFF - Helicopter used to pick up wounded or dead.

GLOSSARY

DZ - Drop Zone, an area where a parachute jump is to be made. Could signify one parachutist or an entire regiment.

EM CLUB - Stands for Enlisted Men's Club (as opposed to NCO or Officer's Club). A bar, pool table, maybe ping-pong table, juke box; a spot for soldiers under the rank of corporal to relax.

E & E - Evade and Escape, a tactic taught most soldiers but especially the Special Forces and SOG teams and the LURPS groups while on a mission of reconnaissance in gathering intelligence. Get in, get the information, and then get out safely and bring the information back to base camp.

EXTRACTION SLICK - Name for any helicopter that will pick up troops who are under heavy enemy fire, to pick up wounded or just pick up a reconnaissance team who has completed or terminated their mission.

FAC - Forward Air Command (or Forward Air Controller) a small reconnaissance aircraft (L-l9 or Bird dog) that flew across the *hot* zones and reported back to the base and would assist troops on the ground and the C & C helicopter by transmitting radio messages.

FINGER CHARGE - Explosive booby-trap device that gets its slang name because it is approximately the size of a man's finger.

FIREBASE - A temporary combat base set up in hostile territory from which patrols are sent out to search for the enemy.

FLASHETTE - A mine without great explosive power containing small pieces of shrapnel intended to wound or kill.

FOOTFALLS - Simple traps built mostly by the VC. They would dig out a small patch of ground, maybe 4 inches below the surface, and line it with sharp *pungi* sticks, then cover them with grass. When walking through the jungles you had to always be alert; there was always the chance of an ambush, trip wires on booby traps to look for or these small holes where you would step and stick sharp stakes (usually dipped in dung to cause infection) through your foot. There were larger traps too, ones dug like a tiger trap, and lined with long, sharp stakes embedded in the ground and covered by a canvas or poncho or tree branches and grass. To fall into one of those was instant death by impalement.

FRAG - A fragmentation grenade, usually homemade by the VC. These grenades had an assortment of steel, glass - anything - that would tear and maim. More often than not they were unreliable, much to the pleasure of those they were being thrown AT.

FREE-FIRE ZONE - An area that is not supposed to contain any allies in which the soldier is *free* to fire at anything. During the early days when the US was not supposed to be in Laos or Cambodia, in the event a Delta or SOG team was in the area, it was a *free-fire zone* for them.

GREEN BERET - A name all members of Special Forces answer to. In reality it is merely a *hat*, but this hat symbol-

GLOSSARY

izes the member of the finest team of combat soldier the world has ever known. The MAROON beret is for Airborne and the BLACK beret is for Airborne Rangers, a qualified, deadly yet different group than Special Forces.

GRUNT - Slang term for infantryman.

GUNSHIP - An attack helicopter, heavily armed with 2 M-60 machine guns, a 6-barrel Gatling gun, some added armor plating and a 36, 48 or 52 cylinder pod for rockets. Used for extractions in "hot" zones. During the course of the war in Vietnam, the United States lost 4,869 helicopters.

H & I - Harassment and Interdiction, commonly called H & I fire. Artillery bombardments used to deny the enemy terrain which they might find beneficial to their campaign. The targets for H & I were general rather than specific, confirmed military targets.

HO CHI MINH SLIPPERS - Sandals made from tires - soles made from the tread, and straps made from inner tubes. Used by many Vietnamese, North and South.

HO CHI MINH TRAIL - A well-known trail that started in North Vietnam and ran along the Anamese Mountains, through Laos and Cambodia and ended in the Mekong Delta in South Vietnam. The NVA and VC used this trail to move men and equipment (food, ammunition, weapons). In 1959 it was truly a *trail* that took close to three months to travel from end to end. By 1975 travel took less than a week.

HOOCH - A Vietnamese jungle or country dwelling for

humans, regardless how primitive. Could be a thatched-roof house, a few boards with tin for a roof or a hole in the side of a mountain with a canopy-type awning in front made of canvas. GI's in Nam often referred to their personal living quarters in the field, maybe their tent with (or without a wooden floor) as their *hooch*.

HOOCHGIRL - Young Vietnamese woman employed by American military as maid and laundress.

HUEY - Yet another name for a *helicopter* or *chopper*. The Huey was a series of helicopters used in Vietnam starting with the HU-7A, UH-1C, UH-1D, etc.

JUNGLE BOOTS - Footwear that looks like a combination boot and canvas sneaker used by the U.S. Military in tropical climates, where leather rots because of the dampness. The canvas structure also speeds in drying after crossing streams, rice paddies, etc.

JUNGLE UTILITIES - Lightweight, tropical fatigues. Combat soldiers had to choose between this lightweight material or the heavier garb that took more abuse from thorns, burrs and the razor-sharp grass and reeds.

KA-BAR - A military knife used by various troops for jungle fighting. Each service had a special knife but the option was with the individual soldier. There were Army and Marine knives, a Navy knife, one used by SEALS, and Special Forces had a knife; some chose to have their knives made, depending on the particular section of jungle, mountain or delta area where they were fighting.

KIA - Killed In Action.

KILLING ZONE - Usually referred to an area within an ambush where people are being killed or wounded.

KIT CARSONS - North Vietnamese who pledged their allegiance to the South. They assisted the Special Forces in gathering intelligence, infiltrating enemy encampments. Many were used as ROADRUNNERS; they would run along the trails dressed in the black pajamas of the VC and give the US reconnaissance information. Again, the main trouble was you never knew which side of the coat they were wearing. They could have feigned their allegiance to us whereas they were actual spies from the North. The majority of the Kit Carson scouts were trustworthy and competent fighters. Some, however, were double-agents.

KLICK - Service term for kilometer; measures out to be a bit over six-tenths of a mile.

LAW - Light anti-tank weapon. A rocket in a disposable tube that allows you one shot. Used for firing on tanks, machine gun emplacements, destroying a hooch or shooting into advancing enemy troops.

LEG - Term used by the airborne to signify a non-jumper, not a *loving term* but rather a macho term. Airborne, they feel, are special.

LT - A term used mostly on the tv series, *Tour of Duty*: Short for lieutenant.

LURPS - Members of Long Range Reconnaissance

Patrols, specially trained combatants who are said to *enjoy danger*. They would gather information, capture an enemy for interrogation, and undertake special missions of demolition and assassination.

LZ - Signifies Landing Zone, a place large enough for a chopper to land and let troops out for combat or reconnaissance.

M-16 - The standard US Infantryman's weapon. A lightweight, manufactured by Colt Firearms. It has a 20 or 30-round belly-clip and fires 5.56 mm bullets. The M-16A1 was fitted with a 40-mm M203 grenade launcher under the barrel, enabling the weapon to propel small-spin stabilized grenades to a range of about 350 meters. Loaded with a 30-round clip, it weighs just a tad over 8 pounds and is the Western World's answer to the AK-47. A simple movement with the thumb can move it from SAFETY, to SEMI-AUTOMATIC, to FULL-AUTO.

MAMA SAN - Used by GI's for any older Vietnamese Woman (*Papa San*, signifying older man).

MERCENARY - A term meaning anyone who fights for money. I was very close to one American mercenary who worked for the CIA and he did, in fact, earn big money. He was trained in all forms of combat, worked with explosives, and was an expert marksman. He worked for the US behind the lines in Cambodia and Laos at a time when our regular troops were *not allowed* to go in. He wanted the rules to be fair and if captured would be treated as a spy, the US disavowing that he worked for them.

MIA - Missing In Action.

MONTAGNARD - Indigenous hill people who fought for money. The Montagnards were not highly respected by the Vietnamese (North or South) and lived mostly in the hills, in primitive fashion in South East Asia. Montagnards (*Yards*) were star pupils of the Special Forces and were tough tribesman who did not think fondly towards ethnic Vietnamese. The one fear many GI's had was you were never certain if they had been hired *by* you or went to top bidder and were already hired by opposing forces. There are several stories that attest both to the bravery and loyalty of these Yards...on both sides! Many GI's owe their lives to some of these Yards and will swear by them.

MPC - Military Payment Certificates; script issued for soldiers to use instead of American money.

NUNGS - These were ethnic Chinese who proved to be truly fierce fighters. In the story of MOH recipient Roger Donolon, the Nungs fought fiercely to defend the position. They were oftentimes referred to as *mercenaries*, not a revered term by many, but everyone gets paid something for war, hmm?

NVA - The North Vietnamese Army, comprised of regular army troops who were as skilled as any, proved a tough, battle-hardened force who had fought against the French and had a winning record. They were *regular* army made up of volunteers who were expert jungle fighters and Vietnam being their home, knew the areas well. They were supplied with top-of-the-line Russian-made weapons and were organized combatants, accustomed to discipline.

OD - Means Olive Drab, for the color of almost everything in the military: trucks, jeeps, tanks, aircraft, Armored Personnel Carriers, tents, uniforms, etc.

POINT-MAN - The first man heading a squad or platoon walking along a trail or through the jungle. The point man (or point) is the first one to encounter mines, booby traps, or the enemy. In an ambush, chances are he'll be shot last...in order to trap the remainder of the squad. It is not, however, a highly revered chore to walk point.

PSEUDOMONAS - A genus of bacteria causing pus in wounds. Its presence gives pus a blue-green color. Found throughout Vietnam but mostly in the wet regions.

PUNGI STAKES - Sharpened ends of tree branches stuck in pitfalls and usually dipped in human excrement to cause instant infection. If not treated quickly, they cause gangrene to set in and result in the need for amputation.

PZ - Initials for a Pickup Zone; the same as an LZ *Landing Zone* and is usually a predetermined spot for ground troops to meet their extraction chopper.

RPG - Rocket Powered Grenade, shot like a bazooka and can be handled by one person. The *grenade* part is in front and looks like a small bomb in the front barrel of a rifle.

R & R - a vacation, one where you get Rest and Relaxation, usually a 3-day pass but can be longer.

SAPPER - A soldier, usually a guerilla (VC) who would invade a base or camp, oftentimes armed with heavy

GLOSSARY

explosives to destroy lives and property. Many *sappers* in Vietnam when shot, simply exploded.

SEAL - Elite combat group of the US Navy (Sea - Air - Land). SEALS were at home in the air, on-or under the water, on-or under land (many SEALS worked as *tunnel rats*). They were taught to avoid or take out the enemy, infiltrate an objective, and carry out their mission. They would gather intelligence, kidnap, sabotage, rescue, or assassinate. Skilled with knives, weapons, and explosives.

SHAPED CHARGE - Any number of explosive charges, the energy of which is focused in one direction. (Claymore)

SHRAPNEL - Term used for any *filler* in an explosive charge. It could be nails, glass, or pieces of metal but usually, the outer core of a shell, mortar round, hand grenade, or metal from a helicopter, truck, jeep...any pieces of metal that fly through the air because of an explosion.

SLICK - A helicopter used to lift troops or equipment, armed with two M-60 doorguns. A Warrant Officer acts as pilot, and another WO as co-pilot. Travels with 2 door gunners (usually enlisted men) and a bellyman who assists with the McGuire Rig and, in combat situations, maybe a medic.

SMASH - Short for Sergeant Major, top sergeant in a battalion or brigade.

SMOKE GRENADE - A grenade that releases brightly colored smoke; used for signaling landing and pickup zones.

SOI PAPERS - Standard Operating Instructions. Usually has 24-hour radio frequencies for patrols needing to be extracted to call the C&C chopper or FAC airplane to direct extraction choppers to the PZ, as well as maps of the area, certain checkpoints for a possible rendezvous with other teams or other information that was classified as to location of camps or troop movement.

TAC - Tactical Air Command (or TAS) that stands for Tactical Air Support. This can mean Air Force, Navy, Marine airplanes or helicopters, or Army gunships that come into a *hot* zone to give air support to troops on the ground. They come in with rockets, bombs, napalm, machine gun, mini-gun or Gatling gun fire and actually *level* the jungle and give our ground troops an opportunity to board an extraction *slick* to safety while the enemy scampers for cover.

TIGER FATIGUES - Government-issue combat pants and shirt/jacket that are camouflaged to blend in with the local terrain. Usual field clothing for Special Forces.

TOP - Short name for First Sergeant of a company.

TRACER - A bullet that has phosphorus at the base of the shell that burns and provides a visual track of the bullet's flight and usually spaced every fifth round. At night, in the open, the tracers look like huge fiery ropes swimming in a curved line in the air.

USOM - United States Operation Mission.

VC - Initials signifying a Vietnamese Communist or *Viet*

GLOSSARY

Cong. These were bands of ragtag guerilla fighters and sometimes skilled volunteers who knew the jungles well. They were from the North (or believed the doctrine of Communism) and tried to force their beliefs on the South Vietnamese. Thus, the reason for the entire war. The frightening part about the VC is that they had no rules. They tortured and killed villagers from the South who even spoke with an American. Yet another frightening fact was you never knew who they were. Many South Vietnamese were drafted (or volunteered) to fight for the North (and vice versa). They could walk around a city crowded with American servicemen undetected. They had no uniforms; they were civilians. Those who fought in the jungles usually donned black pajama-type clothing but in the cities they hired on as mess boys or hoochgirls or worked in the markets and clubs and acted as friendlies, the men and the women; even small children.

VIL - Short for a village indicating any location from a small town or several hundred inhabitants to a gathering of a few thatched-roof huts in a clearing. Mostly, a gathering of country farmers away from a large city.

WILLY PETER - A shell or grenade containing white phosphorous.

XO - The Executive Officer...second in command.

ZAPPED - A term used by combat soldiers that meant shooting someone or getting shot.

I salute you veterans who experienced any of these horrors of war and I hope you - and civilians too - enjoyed this book. If you see some nomenclature errors or descriptions that aren't exactly what you knew them to be, forgive me for it. I researched this information for many months, I spent time both in the U.S. Navy and Army and I had civilians who were friends, historians, and veterans help with this research.

I thank each and every one of you for purchasing this book. I enjoyed writing it and remember, a percentage of the gross from all book sales will go to aid Homeless Vietnam Veterans and to help build the Nurses Memorial.

Pete Billac

TO ORDER THIS BOOK OR OTHER BOOKS BY
PETE BILLAC, WRITE TO:

SWAN PUBLISHERS
PO Box 580242
Houston, TX 77258

FOR CREDIT CARD ORDERS, CALL 1-800-933-3939
QUANTITY DISCOUNTS AVAILABLE